D1600830

UNDERCOVER ASSIGNMENT

Gunn awoke suddenly. Someone had pulled his blanket away from him. In the dim light he saw only the outline of someone's form.

"Mister Gunn."

Christina's whisper fell hot on his ear. Her wheat-blond hair shimmered around her face like silk in the moon's pewter light.

"What in hell are you doing here?"

"I need to be near you tonight."

She knelt down and slipped the cotton nightgown from her shoulders. Then she was under the blanket snuggling close, her breasts soft against his chest. The young woman's heat, the smell of her musk, made Gunn giddy with want. He sucked in his breath, wrapped his arms around her body, brushed his mouth against her lips.

"You make it hard on a man," he said.

"Show me how it feels, Gunn," she said, pressing her loins into his. "Show me just how hard it feels."

GREAT WESTERNS
by Dan Parkinson

THE SLANTED COLT   (1413, $2.25)
A tall, mysterious stranger named Kichener gave young Benjamin Franklin Blake a gift. It was a gun, a colt pistol, that had belonged to Ben's father. And when a cold-blooded killer vowed to put Ben six feet under, it was a sure thing that Ben would have to learn to use that gun — or die!

GUNPOWDER GLORY   (1448, $2.50)
Jeremy Burke, breaking a deathbed promise to his pa, killed the lowdown Sutton boy who was the cause of his pa's death. But when the bullets started flying, he found there was more at stake than his own life as innocent people were caught in the crossfire of *Gunpowder Glory*.

BLOOD ARROW   (1549, $2.50)
Randall Kerry returned to his camp to find his companion slaughtered and scalped. With a war cry as wild as the savages', the young scout raced forward with his pistol held high to meet them in battle.

BROTHER WOLF   (1728, $2.95)
Only two men could help Lattimer run down the sheriff's killers — a stranger named Stillwell and an Apache who was as deadly with a Colt as he was with a knife. One of them would see justice done — from the muzzle of a six-gun.

CALAMITY TRAIL   (1663, $2.95)
Charles Henry Clayton fled to the west to make his fortune, get married and settle down to a peaceful life. But the situation demanded that he strap on a six-gun and ride toward a showdown of gunpowder and blood that would send him galloping off to either death or glory on the . . . *Calamity Trail*.

BY JORY SHERMAN

FRONTIER FANNY #24

GUNN

ZEBRA BOOKS

KENSINGTON PUBLISHING CORP.

ZEBRA BOOKS

are published by

Kensington Publishing Corp.
475 Park Avenue South
New York, NY 10016

First printing: February 1986

Printed in the United States of America

For Veronica F., a lady in waiting.

Chapter One

Deep in the big oak's foliage, a single small branch quivered under the weight of the great horned owl. Its throaty call floated eerily over the nightscape, echoed in the canyon where the three wagons, set together like wooden elephants, tongues touching the boxes like stiffened trunks, stood shrouded in the silvered darkness. At the center of the makeshift breastworks, the glow of the dying cookfire flicked shadows, licked streaks of light on the blanketed lumps of sleeping travelers. The owl called again, its bass notes proclaiming the bird's presence, its territory.

The owl's hoot was the only sound in the prairie stillness.

Gunn felt himself floating upward through layers of sleep-haze, rising out of dream against his will, as if summoned. He opened his gray-blue eyes, fixed on the glowing fire. Night was still thick beyond the tiny circle of feeble light. The stars were cockeyed, shifted from their earlier position. He glanced at the horizon, but there was no rent in the fabric of night, no pale pink dawn as a harbinger of day. He stretched

7

under the blanket, cracking leg joints. His bones ached and he knew that for some reason his rest had been cut short.

The owl made no sound as it flew from its perch in the dusky oak, but he heard the heavy wings beating the air overhead, saw its dark silhouette wipe out a path through the stars. Then, in its wake, a heavy silence, as if the earth itself was holding its breath.

He listened.

Except for the soft snore from one of the bundles, and a faint crackle from the fire's embers, there was no sound. Odd. There was no scurry of small animal paws in the brush, no insect sound. Only the eerie empty silence that cloaked the campsite. Even the horses were quiet. They had stopped feeding, did not move under hobbled restraints.

Something was damned sure wrong.

There was not a breath of air. But in his skull, the silence roared like a windstorm in a seashell.

Gunn raised himself up on one elbow, moving slowly and carefully. He felt for the Winchester '73 with his left hand.

A horse whickered in the trees and Gunn's muscles tautened like a tuned drumhead. His nerves twanged like a suddenly broken guitar string.

Bedded down some distance from the wagons, his bedroll laid out on a high knoll overlooking the campsite, Gunn scanned the clearing for signs of life. He saw only the sleeping forms, the wagons, the circle of stones, the pulsing coals, the shimmering light at the center of the firepit.

Everything seemed normal. Still, he drew the rifle out from under his blanket, ran a palm up the barrel.

There was no dew on its blued steel. It was warm from his body.

Gunn relaxed as his fingers touched the wood of the stock, oddly comforting in the darkness.

Imagination could play tricks on a man at such times.

He almost laughed. Perhaps, he thought, the hunting owl had driven the night critters to ground, hushed them with his beating wings.

He set the rifle down, but did not slide it under the blanket. Just in case. He stretched out in the bedroll, threw an arm across his forehead.

Maybe I should put on my boots, he thought, as he closed his eyes.

It hit him then. The fire. He had told the people to put it out or they might not make Fort Phil. Instead, they had let it burn, let it die down, sending the smell of smoke all over the damned country like an engraved invitation.

Gunn jerked upright, pulled his boots out from under his saddleblanket pillow. He tugged them on, cursing the people down there who had not listened to his orders. They might as well have put up a sign as to leave that fire going.

Something had damned sure made that owl leave its perch. There was nothing to hunt in this small box canyon.

The owl had been settling down in its daytime home, waiting for the dawn. Warning all other creatures that this was his territory.

Gunn almost missed it.

He rolled out of the blankets, strapped on his gunbelt, grabbed up his hat and the Winchester.

He stayed low, against the bank above the knoll, so that he would make no silhouette. He started to make his circle around the camp, check the oak from where the owl had flown, the clump of cottonwoods beyond, above the little creek that threaded through the low, rolling hills.

The owl hooted again.

But this time, it was not a true owl.

Gunn went into a crouch, grabbed the lever of the Winchester.

Too late.

A savage war-cry rose from the trees beyond the circle of wagons. Mounted horsemen burst from cover, rode wildly up to the wagons. Expertly, the Indians slid the tongues from the boxes, rode into the camp, brandishing weapons. Rifles cracked. Orange blossoms of flame spouted from muzzles. Pistols boomed. Puffs of white smoke hung in the darkness like miniature clouds. The acrid bite of burnt black powder stung Gunn's nostrils.

A woman shrieked. The horses reared up, whinnying in high-pitched terror. They tried to bolt toward the wagons, but their hobbles made them flounder like creatures caught in a swamp bog. A wagon caught fire. Streaks of flame lashed from the blankets, and Gunn saw a half-naked brave throw up his arms and pitch from the back of his spotted pony.

Gunn braced himself against the bank, picked a target. He jacked a shell into the chamber, tracked a buck on foot as he stalked toward one of the blankets, war-stick raised overhead for striking *coup*. He squeezed the trigger, saw the man go down before the smoke blotted him out.

A bullet fried the air near Gunn's head. A shiver, cold and sharp, laden with a thousand needles, rippled down his backbone. He dropped to one knee to fire at a mounted shadow beyond the camp circle.

Concentrating on his target, Gunn did not see the rider sweeping toward him on his blind side.

Something crashed into the side of his head.

Twisting, he saw a dark form float past him. The stars spun, danced madly overhead. His skull throbbed with pain.

He felt the darkness close over him as all the dancing lights went out.

Light shimmered above him, out of focus. Gunn's head throbbed with an ache that threatened to blind him. He fought to keep his eyes open. He moved his head and knew it was a mistake. Pain seared through his temples, flowed down his neck like molten lava. With great effort he lifted his head. His skull felt as if it would burst as he raised himself to his elbows and gagged. The taste of sour bile filled his throat. His nose stung with the stench of blood.

Gunn struggled to rise. Black waves of nausea rolled in on him like a prairie storm. He twisted onto his hands and knees like a drunk after a barroom brawl, staggered to his feet.

Somewhere, through the whirring rush in his ears, he heard a crackling sound. He stumbled forward, trying to focus his eyes. The crackling continued. Not bullets. Fire. Except for the popping of the flames, a deathly silence laced the darkness.

The wagons blazed with a fury, painting the night

11

orange. Wisps of clouds floated past a pale moon, bathing the campsite in an eerie glow of silverdust.

Gunn smelled death as he staggered toward the wagons. He tripped over an open trunk and in his effort to regain his balance, swore. His head drummed with pain.

Clothes and household goods littered the ground. Then Gunn saw the bodies. Men and women sprawled at terrible angles, sightless. Fire shadows flickered on their faces fixed in death stares. Bullet holes punctured throats, chests. Dried blood decorated shirts and bodices. Pieces of meat that had been living flesh littered the ground.

Nausea gripped Gunn like a vise. He retched again. His gut rumbled as he reeled, struggled to hold down the bile rising in his throat. He stood for a time trying to focus on the nightmare. The scene of horror.

The mules and oxen were gone, driven off. A horse nickered from somewhere in the trees. Esquire. Gunn remembered that he had hobbled his horse to graze in the safety of the woods.

Gunn lurched toward the sound of the whicker. Another sound stopped him in his tracks. A low, soft sound. A moan. It came from somewhere beneath one of the wagons. Gunn turned to listen. It came again, floating quietly on the night air. Near the tongue of the far wagon.

A buckskin-covered arm moved slightly as Gunn approached the burning wagon box. "Jacques. Jacques Laurent." Gunn spoke to himself, his own pain forgotten as he pulled the dying man away from the roasting flames.

"Willow. Green Willow Leaf. Is she all right?"

12

Jacque's words came hard from the bleeding man.

"I haven't seen her, Jacques."

"Look for her, Gunn. Please."

Gunn crawled toward a white-clad figure lying near the wagon wheel. The deerskin dress of Jacques' wife looked like plaster in a death-cast. A wave of nausea churned through Gunn's stomach as he rolled the woman's body over. It was the Cheyenne woman, Green Willow Leaf.

Gunn slipped his arm under the shoulders of the woman and lifted her body to him. The head lolled back like a rag doll. Her neck was broken. The rust of dried blood caked the bronzed face, the shiny black hair. Black eyes, glazed in death, stared into the night.

"Jacques, where's Fanny?" Gunn had not seen Laurent's half-breed daughter, Francine.

"Taken. Alive. You must find her."

"The Indians took her?"

Jacques coughed, blood bubbling in his throat. His breath labored as he spoke again. "They took her. Not Indians."

"Not Indians?" Gunn remembered savage screams before his lights had gone out.

"White men. I know him. Jack Blood. Bad. Real bad." Jacques' eyes fluttered. Death was creeping in on him. "Gunn. Find her. Find Fanny. Give her this." The Frenchman pressed something into Gunn's hand.

Gunn opened his palm toward the firelight. A lick of flames illuminated the beaded necklace in Gunn's hand. It belonged to Green Willow Leaf. The Cheyenne woman's blood coated the amulet.

"Bring her. . . ." Jacques' words rushed out on his

last breath. The hoar-frost of death glazed his eyes.

Gunn's jaw hardened. "I'll find her for you, Jacques." He spoke softly now. It didn't matter. His friend couldn't hear him.

Pocketing the necklace, Gunn repeated his promise.

"I'll find her, Jacques."

Chapter Two

Picking gingerly through the crimson rubble, Gunn found a half-burned shovel. Its handle still smoked. He tapped the implement against a nearby tree to remove the hot, charred wood. Enough of the tool was left to do the painful task ahead of him.

Gunn tamped the ground around him until he found a spot soft enough to begin digging. The smoldering wagons lit the tall man's excavation site. The grave would have to be big enough to accommodate the six bodies which lay around him. There wasn't enough time or energy for six separate graves.

Pain throbbed through Gunn's head as he dug. Sweat glistened on his forehead, dripping salt into his eyes. Nausea boiled once more in his gut.

Later, when the digging was complete, Gunn dragged the bodies, one by one, and laid them in the wide, shallow crater he had made. Covering the grave with dirt and stones, he left no marker. Finding Jack Blood would be the only marker these folks needed.

Dawn spread a wide salmon streak across the sky as Gunn made ready for the trail. He found extra jerky and a spare canteen among Jacques' belongings. He loaded Esquire with the two water containers, an extra set of saddlebags for food, placed his bedroll behind the saddle and filled his own saddlebags with as much ammunition as he could find for his Winchester '73 and Colt .45. The drygulchers had been careless. They had not tarried long enough to rummage through all the belongings. Gunn had enough supplies to track Blood's gang to hell if he had to.

Gunn mounted his Tennessee Walker and began to skirt the campsite, checking the tracks. He had to be sure of the number and direction of the murderers. His eyes strained in the morning light, but he shook off the agony, the weariness. Fanny's life depended on him.

The sorrel horse drifted, walking stiff-legged, its ears perked, eyes wild in their sockets, circling the smoldering wagons. The ground was littered with tracks and empty rifle shells glistening in the first rays of light. The sun began to warm the rider's back as he tried to make sense out of the scramble of hoofprints. The runaway stock only added confusion to the maze of tracks on the ground. Still, Gunn circled the camp, widening his path with each circuit.

The tracker watched closely for tell-tale signs, dismounting often to examine the earth more closely. Soon he sorted out the hoofprints that led away from camp. There was nothing particularly distinctive about the tracks. Following the trail slowly for some time, Gunn was finally able to sort out the sign of eight riders on shod mounts and about a dozen stock horses. The prints were deep for seven of the riders,

16

light for the eighth. The horse packing light was freshly shod. It would be the one carrying Fanny.

The sun was up hot now, boiling the air. Heat waves rose in the distance. Gunn spurred Esquire alongside the tracks and made better time for awhile. The trail led through ravines and dry creek beds. Topping a rise, Gunn stopped Esquire and dismounted. His rumbling gut reminded him that he had not eaten since before the massacre. He removed a piece of jerky from his saddlebag, slowly chewed a salty chunk as he gazed across the rolling land. Fanny was out there somewhere. That half-grown woman whom everyone liked so well. Fanny was out there with a murderer who Gunn knew only as Jack Blood.

Suddenly Esquire sidestepped, whinnied. The horse pranced, perked his ears and fought the bit. Gunn spoke to his mount, keeping his voice low and calm. The animal's nostrils flared, twitched.

Gunn remounted and stood in his stirrups, trying to pick up the scent, the sound or the sight that had spooked the horse. He looked ahead, scanned the grassland. A dark, ominous shape broke the rhythm of the grama grass.

Clucking to the horse, Gunn tapped spurs without rowels into the animal's flanks. The drygulchers' tracks headed toward the distant speck. Keeping the mound in sight, man and beast circled to keep the sun at their backs.

The form took shape. It was a horse, a pinto, down. Gunn reined Esquire in as close as the spooked Walker dared to go and dismounted. The pinto was dead, still saddled, its carcass beginning to swell and stink. Gunn looked skyward, surprised that buzzards had not begun to gather. Walking around to the head of the carcass, Gunn noticed one clean shot between the pinto's eyes. A man wouldn't shoot a horse on the prairie without good reason. He checked the horse's hoofs and noticed a splintered fetlock. The pinto had pulled up lame. Probably stepped in a gopher hole.

There was something else about the animal. The shoes showed only slight wear. This must be the same mount that Fanny had been riding, the fresh-shod one. Gunn walked the trampled grass around the carcass for sign. Bootheels marked the broken grass blades and soft earth. Walking further, he noticed that seven animals' tracks headed north, not the eight he had been following. Fanny was riding double. It would be hard to tell which horse she rode now. Deeper hoofprints could indicate two passengers or one large man.

Catching up his horse, Gunn mounted and followed the seven sets of tracks. The sun was high by now as the horse and rider continued their trek. After several hours, the trail led into a ravine. The renegades had stopped to rest and eat. A small circle of rocks and black ash bespoke of coffee brewed. The fire ring was too small and too old for a meat fire. Likely the gang ate jerky, washing it down with hot coffee. Gunn could drink a tin of the hot, black liquid about now, but time was short. Fanny needed help and the drygulchers couldn't be more than six, maybe eight hours ahead of him. Stopping for rest or coffee would eat up time he didn't have. He swabbed a dusty bandanna across his forehead, flexed his muscles. The tall man's shadow was shrinking up short as the sun moved toward its zenith.

Gunn satisfied his thirst with a gulp of water and clucked at Esquire to move on. Out on the flat again, Gunn reined his mount in and studied a curious crisscrossing of tracks. The renegades had split into two groups. Four horses continued north while the other three veered to the west. Which group had Fanny?

She must be with the northbound men. It would take one man to guard the girl and three for defense. Either way, it would be Gunn against three or four rifles.

The man and the Walker continued north toward the Bozeman Trail. The bloody Bozeman. The forts along the trail had been under constant seige from Sioux and Cheyenne for more than a year. Chief Red Cloud and his Sioux harassed Fort Phil Kearny and Fort C.F. Smith on the Bighorn River north of Fort Phil Kearney. Sometimes the skirmishes occurred daily with but a few casualties on each side. Some fights became battles with the loss of dozens of Indians and soldiers. The Sioux and Cheyenne did not limit their killing to the cavalry. They attacked anyone who got in the way. Wagons full of settlers were often wiped out, scalped, their meager stores looted.

Gunn would have to be alert, but not appear to be in any hurry or going any place in particular. It would give him an advantage, time to react in case of trouble. It wasn't likely that Indians would waste their time on a lone drifter. The horse and rider began a plodding gait across the flats.

The sky began to smudge in the west. The clouds turned pink, then purpled as the sun sank from the horizon. The Walker stepped easy along the trail, its rider nodding in the saddle. Suddenly the horse's ears pricked, then stood stiff, alert. Esquire halted and whickered, rousing Gun from his torpor. The horse's nostrils flared at the new scent. The rider scanned his surroundings, his spine rippling with an involuntary shiver.

"What's the matter, boy? You smell Indians?" Gunn sniffed the air, too, not sure of what he smelled.

"Bacon. By god, Esquire, that's bacon cooking." He spurred the horse gently, seeking the direction of the mouth-watering aroma.

Capping a small rise, Gunn found the source of the pungent odor. Five wagons tightly circled a campfire at the edge of a creekbed just below him.

A man called out, "Rider coming in."

"Hello the camp!" Gunn responded, raising his arms to show empty palms.

"Keep 'em up there, mister, and ride in nice and easy."

Gunn couldn't see who spoke, but did as he was told.

"Hold it right there," the same man said as Gunn neared the circle. "Git down and tie that horse to a wagon tongue with your off hand. Keep your shooting hand high."

Gunn continued to follow orders until he saw a bandy-legged old man step from the shadow of a wagon.

"You can't blame a man for riding up on you," Gunn said. "Just headed this way when I smelled the bacon frying."

The old man chuckled, lowering the rifle he had aimed at Gunn's chest. "Heh. Heh. Don't blame you ary bit. Old Buffaler Woman is about the best cook in these parts. Name's Ben Walters. That there Buffaler Woman is my squaw." The man gestured to a portly Indian woman who squatted by the fire, then offered his hand to Gunn. "Who you be, stranger?"

"Gunn," the tall man replied, shaking the man's hand. His name didn't seem to register with the codger. "Where you folks headed?"

Ben gestured for Gunn to step into the wagon fortress. "Sorry I throwed down on you. We'uns is headed for Fort Phil Kearny. Hope to get there with our hair in place. I reckon everybody here is as nervous as a long-tailed cat in a roomful of rockers. Them danged Injuns are kicking up a ruckus all up and down the Bozeman. We just heard about the Sioux and Cheyenne joining together and attacking the fort a few days ago. And some riders on the trail today said that the Oglallas and Cheyennes attacked it again last night. We all stuck together hoping to get to the safety of the soldiers." A clatter of pans caused the old man to jerk his rifle toward the fire. "I reckon I'm as skittish as the rest of 'em. Where you headed?"

"Looking for a man," Gunn replied.

"Well, iffen you ain't too particular, there's one here I'd be obliged if you take off our hands."

Gunn chuckled. "Got a problem?"

"Ain't so much a problem as he is a worthless drawback. Young feller, Higgins. Stays drunk all the time. Shame, too. And him with such a pretty sister. That's her, Christina, climbing down outta that wagon over yonder."

21

The steel-gray eyes flickered as Gunn looked at the young woman. Christina Higgins stepped from the shadow of the wagon into the dusky firelight. She was small, dainty, with long blond hair that melted over her shoulders. Her plain cotton dress could not disguise the high, firm breasts that pressed against the faded fabric. Her waist was tiny, so small Gunn figured he could circle it with his hands. Her skirt fell smoothly over rounded hips. Gunn felt a warm stirring in his loins as he watched the young woman approach the fire. His eyes fixed on her across the circle. She had blue eyes that crackled like sunlight on a high lake. She nodded slightly in acknowledgment of his look as he touched two fingers to his hat brim.

From somewhere in a wagon, a baby whimpered, bringing Gunn's attention back to Ben Walters.

"You said there were riders today. A young girl with them?"

"Naw. Just some of Jack Blood's men headed to the Fort. Don't know how they knew about the attack last night. They were coming from the wrong direction. Come up from the south."

"Jack Blood. That's the man I'm looking for," Gunn replied.

Ben let out a long breath. "You're after a pack of trouble, Mister Gunn. That half-breed is an outcast. The Sioux drove him out and the whites treat him like a dog. He wants the treaty broken. He attacked a bunch of Cheyenne on the Otter. Wearin' soldier blue, he was. Now them Injuns think the troopers at Phil Kearny want to make war. Blood's men said the Injuns massacred a wagon train last night."

"There was a train massacred all right. I was with

22

them. But it wasn't Indians. It was Blood and his men. They took a young girl. Her father was my friend. He's dead now." Gunn paused. "How many men came by today?"

"Four was all I seed."

"Damn. I took the wrong trail. Should've turned west."

"You been riding since daybreak, you need rest. Bed down with us tonight. Buffaler Woman'll be glad to rustle you up some vittles."

Gunn was about to reject the offer when a scream shrilled from the Higgins' wagon.

A woman's scream.

Chapter Three

The scream jarred Gunn's senses. He bounded across the clearing, barely skirting the fire, instinctively snatching at his holstered .45.

Gunn, as he reached the wagon, heard the open-handed slap of flesh against flesh. He used the barrel of his pistol to move the canvas covering of the wagon just enough to see inside.

A candle flickered atop a bureau on the near side of the wagon. Its dancing light allowed Gunn to view the back of a small-built man. Nervous shadows enlarged the swinging arm that landed blows on someone unseen. Gunn cocked the Colt, swept the curtain aside.

"Hold it right there," he said, leveling the gun at the assailant's back.

The man who turned to face Gunn was hardly a man at all. He was young, handsome and lean. No farmer or settler. The hint of dark sideburns framed a finely chiseled face. His clothes looked tailored, well-kept. With his striking hand still aloft, the man-boy staggered back slightly as he faced Gunn.

"Let her go." Gunn's voice was firm. The barrel of his pistol held steady on the man's belt buckle.

"Do as he says, Steve. He's not fooling." Christina's voice quavered through bleeding lips. The tracks of tears streaked her face. Her brother's hand still gripped a knot of cloth at the neck of her dress.

"Min' your own business, mister," Steve Higgins slurred, his speech thick-tongued from too much whiskey. Trying to focus red eyes on Gunn, the dandy began to sway, fell back on his haunches. The gingham at the girl's throat ripped down to her waist. One of her breasts dropped into view.

"Any man who beats a woman is my business. Now ease on over toward me and step down out of the wagon." The young man was unarmed, but Gunn wanted to be sure. The man could have a weapon handy among his belongings.

"Can I bring my bottle?" The man's voice turned into that of a boy as he gestured toward a corked flask that lay among the quilts on the cot at the front of the wagon.

"Bring it and get out of there." Gunn watched the kid stumble for the bottle and scramble over the household goods in a drunken effort to retrieve his whiskey. Clambering over the tailgate of the weapon, the drunkard pitched headlong onto the ground at Gunn's feet. The boy groaned, sat up, uncorked the bottle and began to suck on its contents.

Gunn shoved the Colt back in its holster, stepped over the backboard, and sat beside the girl. He dabbed at her bloody lips with the torn collar of her dress. She closed her swollen eyes and moaned softly. She opened her eyes again. Gunn looked into their

26

blue depths, winced inside. She had a look and it tore at him, but he didn't know why. She was just beautiful, and she had so much heartache. He wished he had taken the other trail.

"Steve's not always like that," she said. "He's my brother, all I've got left . . ." Christina lowered her head. Gunn cupped her chin, forced her to look into his eyes. She drew a sudden breath and her chest swelled. "Who are you, anyway?"

"They call me Gunn. Now, shhh," he hissed. He dabbed at the flecks of blood on her lips. "Where are you bound?"

"Virginia City. Bannack."

"Just you and your brother? Your folks . . ."

Tears welled up in her eyes. "They died on the trail. Of the fever. We buried them near Fort Reno." The tears coursed down her cheeks.

"How old are you?"

"Seventeen. Steve's nineteen. He hates the trail, the dust, everything about the west. I guess that's why he drinks so much. It wasn't so bad at first, but now he stays drunk most of the time. He won't listen to me anymore." She stopped talking abruptly as they both heard a loud moan outside the wagon.

Gunn leaned out to see Steve Higgins stagger and collapse against a wagon wheel.

"Your brother passed out," he said.

"Mister Gunn, would you please help me get him up here and into bed. It'll get awfully cold out there tonight."

"Might," he said. Liquor drinking was no good on such a trail. A man needed his senses. Weather could put water in the boy's lungs, make him sick. Gunn

27

had seen men die trying to stay warm with whiskey.

"Please." She jarred him with the softness of her voice, the pleading tone.

He stepped down from the wagon and scooped the young man into his arms. Steve's mouth fell open as Gunn hefted him into the wagon and set his limp body on a cot. Once the man was settled, he began to snore. The sound rasped and buzzed like a wasp trapped in a sulphur matchbox.

"Mister Gunn, will you stay—stay with us tonight? In our wagon?" She leaned forward and her bodice opened wide so that he could see her breast again, the smooth flesh of her bare chest. The bumpy circle of her aureola pulsed in the candlelight. Dark as leather, the patch served to emphasize the startling whiteness of her skin, the beauty of her breast with its matching brown-pink nipple.

"I reckon that might not be proper."

"Please. I'm so scared. Steve—when he gets like this, he does things . . . he beats me."

"He'll be out cold for most of the night. I'll be close by. He hurts you, call out."

Gunn dropped down from the wagon into a camp that had settled down for the night. The Indian woman was the only one moving about. She shuffled toward him, a plate of beans cradled in her hands. "Eat." The fat woman handed him the plate. She turned, left without another word, leaving Gunn alone.

The hot beans, cold bacon and biscuits tasted good to the man who had not eaten much that day. He squatted near the fire, watched the candlelight dancing on the canvas of the Higgins wagon. The outline

28

of Christina's movements wavered as she removed her clothing. Shadows profiled her naked body. She lowered a loose-fitting garment over her head.

Gunn stood up, leaving the empty plate on the ground. He tried to shake off the images lingering in his mind. Beauty was not a thing a man could bury easily, and Christina, undressing, had been beautiful. As Laurie, his dead wife had been beautiful. He had not meant to pry, but he had seen something that stirred long-dormant memories.

Gunn threw his bedroll down, outside the circle of wagons. In the dark, he shucked off his boots. Weariness seeped through his muscles as he crawled under his blanket, tucked his gunbelt underneath for a pillow. He fell asleep in minutes, sank deep in slumber.

Sometime later, he awoke suddenly.

Someone pulled his blanket away from him. He tensed, slid a hand toward his Colt. It was pitch dark, and he saw only the outline of someone's form.

"Mister Gunn."

Christina's whisper fell hot on his ear.

"What in hell are you doing here?" He bolted upright, groggy from being awakened. Her wheat-blond hair shimmered around her face like silk in the dim light.

"I need to be near you tonight." She knelt beside him like some water nymph, slipped under the blankets, and sidled next to him. He felt her heat, smelled her musk. A bare leg burned hot against his.

"Do you know what you're doing?" Gunn husked. The young woman's heat soaked into his loins, the smell of her made him giddy with want. The pale moon floated gaunt-white, luminous, from behind a wisp of cloud.

The girl nodded, slipped her cotton nightgown off her shoulders. Her firm, young nipples jutted erect, taut as tiny thumbs. She snuggled close, her breasts pressing into his chest. Gunn sucked in his breath and wrapped his arms around her body. He looked into her eyes, shimmering with the silvery dust-light from the moon, saw the traces of blue in their sudden-clear depths. A shiver raced through him as he brushed his mouth against her bruised lips. She embraced him with soft arms. Her breath fanned his face with the scent of crushed mint, cinnamon, cloves.

"You make it hard on a man," he said.

"Show me how it feels, Gunn." She pressed her loins into his, crushing his swelling manhood against her hips. She slipped the gown to her feet, kicked it free.

He drew her closer, kissed her again.

"Have you been with a man before?"

Christina stiffened in his arms. "No, not like this. Steve . . . he . . . he fumbles around sometimes when he's drunk. I'm not sure if he knows what he's doing. Then he . . . beats me." Tears brimmed her eyes, coursed down her cheeks in tiny rivers, glistened soft in the moon's pewter light.

Gunn touched a finger to one cheek, then the other, wiping the salty liquid from her face. His mouth traced the path his finger had taken to her cheeks. He peppered her neck, her shoulders, her breasts with light, tongue-stinging kisses. He mouthed a breast; his tongue danced circles around the hardened nipple, slid across the bumps of her

30

aureoles. He felt her tremble in his arms.

He kissed her mouth, slid his tongue into the warm, soft cavern. His loins roiled with the liquid flame of primodial desire. He took her hand, placed it on his hardened stalk. The denim of his trousers stretched tight across his crotch. She drew her hand away, quick as a startled bird.

"I'm scared, Gunn," she whispered. "I've never felt like this before. I ache down there, inside me. I'm quivering inside. Steve made it all so . . . so dirty. He—he hurt me."

"I won't hurt you," Gunn replied. "We can stop now. Better if we did. You have some growing to do."

"No," she said quickly. "I can't stop now. I want you."

"Sure?" He wanted her, but he sensed she was trouble. Any woman was trouble, but this one worried him more than most.

"I want you, Gunn. Please."

She worked at his belt with frantic fingers, unbuttoned his trousers.

"I'll do that," he said with finality, forcing her hand away.

The girl watched the man disrobe in the moonlight.

"Oh, it's so big," she half-whispered as he slid his shorts down his legs. His manhood jutted from his loins like a thick scimitar.

She leaned over, kissed him. "I want you, Gunn. I want this." Her hand grasped his swollen cock, squeezed it, stroked it up and down its bulging length. She swung her hips over his loins. He felt the moist heat of her sex-cleft meld into his groin. His manhood throbbed, swelled with engorged blood, turned rock-hard.

She moaned, squirmed with pleasure, need. He drew her close in a strong embrace, felt her breasts burrow hard against his chest. He rolled her over, shadowed her with his naked frame.

Her legs spread wide, her hips undulating with lust. With her hands she guided his stalk into her tight, velvet sheath. He felt the soft hairs of her thatch rub against his cock. A slow moan escaped her lips. "Take me," she murmured. "Now."

Slowly, gently, he burrowed his shaft into her moist, slick tunnel, plumbing toward her maidenhead. He drove deeper. There was no obstacle in his path. She was not a virgin.

He plunged to the depths of her soft, yielding treasure, filling her with his thickness. Her legs encircled his body as she bucked with the first spasm of unbridled pleasure. Her fingers gripped deep into his shoulders as the orgasm shuddered through her like thunder.

"God, don't stop, Gunn. You're the first real man I've known. Keep doing it. Don't stop." Her voice grew loud above the sounds of smacking flesh.

Gunn placed his mouth over hers; his tongue and his cock kept time with their rocking bodies. Her cunt muscles flexed with a matching rhythm and the two became one motion, one flesh.

He stroked her fast at first, relishing every wild rage of her orgasms. Sliding in and out to meet her every wave, her every moan.

She brought her legs down from around his hips and dug her heels into the blanket. He slid his hands under her rounded hips, drew her up to him and felt the moisture of her dew drip from the puffed lips of her love cavern.

"Yes," she moaned. "Deeper, harder. Oh, Gunn." Her hands rubbed over his back, his neck, through his hair. Her breasts smacked his chest. She rose higher with each orgasm.

She grabbed his buttocks with both her hands as he felt his own tide of pleasure begin to stir deep in his scrotum. He slowed his stroking to savor the heights of their coupling. Slowing, he drove into her, deep and hard. She rolled and thrashed with animal pleasure. He felt himself coming, coming fast. He exploded inside with a rush, his seed spewing to the depths of her womanhood.

He fell atop her, spent.

Softly stroking his sweat-slick body with her dainty hands, she whispered, "Please don't leave me tomorrow, Gunn. I can't go it alone. I'm scared."

He rolled away and lay beside her, gazing up at the stars that played hide-and-seek with the clouds.

He was empty inside, sated. The woman wanted much, gave much. The emptiness was in him. He let out a breath, knowing there was no easy way to let her down.

"You'll be fine, Christina. You're a woman now. Nobody can frighten you anymore. Besides, there's something I have to do. Maybe I'll see you down the trail."

Chapter Four

Gunn figured Jack Blood was a hundred miles or more ahead of him by now. Three, maybe four days hard ride.

The sun painted salmon stripes across the pale sky as Gunn finished saddling the sorrel. The tall man turned as someone walked up behind him.

"Gunn, why don't you ride on to the fort with us? We got plenty of grub. Besides it wouldn't hurt to have another rifle along. What with the Injuns and all."

"No, Ben. I've got something to do," said Gunn. "A promise I made." He rattled the flap down on the cinch ring. Every time he thought of the dead ones, his anger rose in him. Every time he thought of Fanny being held prisoner, he burned. If he let up on Blood, he might . . . but, he didn't want to think of that. He knew how old she was. He knew what a man who killed in cold blood might do to a young woman. Especially one he had murdered to get.

The old man chuckled. "Looks like to me you had something to do last night. Well, I likes the women myself, now and again. But they never come after me like that 'un did with you. Oh, I seen her sneak back to her wagon awhile ago. Ain't no skin offen my back."

Gunn said nothing.

"At least take some grub with you." The old codger handed Gunn a cloth bundle. "There's a pinch of coffee and some hardtack in there."

"Much obliged, Ben." Gunn accepted the food, stowed it in a saddlebag and swung up into the saddle. He squared his felt hat, bent the brim downward. "Maybe see you down the trail, Ben. Keep an eye on the skyline and watch your hair."

"You be careful, too, pilgrim," the old man answered. "Jack Blood, he's smarter'n any white tracker and he always covers his back trail."

Gunn spurred Esquire into an easy gait, backtracking to pick up the trail that would lead him to Fanny Laurent and Jack Blood.

The prairie sun beat down on the lone rider. The incessant, erratic winds sent dust eddies swirling along the trail. Heat waves shimmered over the grassy plain. The horseman followed the meandering wheel ruts made by hundreds of men before him.

A yellow smear of dust appeared on the horizon, causing Esquire to blow a riffle of air through his nostrils and flick his head. The horse halted, stamped the ground with his forefoot.

Gunn peered into the distance, sighted the growing dust trail. "Easy, boy, easy." The rider kept his voice low and even. He leaned forward, patted the anxious animal, never taking his eyes off the billowing cloud.

A white battalion flag appeared out of the haze,

followed by a column of blue-uniformed riders. Cavalry.

Soldiers would take too much time, ask too many questions of a lone horseman. The sound of hoofbeats built to a crescendo as Gunn reined his nervous mount into a nearby draw and dismounted. He snubbed the horse to a stunted tree. The slanting rays of the early afternoon sun left a slice of shade on the west side of the gully.

Esquire grazed the sweet grasses growing in the protected draw while Gunn leaned against the earthen wall munching jerky and hardtack. The thunder passed by, and Gunn's teeth gritted on the floating dust. He drew a breath, pulled his hat brim down and closed his eyes as the thudding sound of pounding hooves faded to an empty silence.

The sun dropped lower in the sky; Gunn, dozing, shook off sleep, peered over the rim of the draw. The plain was empty, the dust cloud gone. He caught up Esquire. The horse was no longer spooked. Refreshed from his nap, Gunn drank from his canteen, wiped his brow of sweat.

The solitary man continued his trek, heading for some low hills in the distance that would offer cover for the night.

Gunn kept the horse going at a slow, ground-eating lope, despite the heat. The country was dangerous now. The treaty was broken. There would be more soldiers on patrol, he was sure, maybe Indian scouting parties as well.

He rode into a valley, an open space cut through by a trickle of a creek that once had been a mighty river. He paused to water his animal, fill his canteen, then crossed the sandy bed over wide flat stones bleached by the sun.

A rifle-shot cracked the air some great distance away.

Gunn topped the rise out of the creek bed in time to see a buckboard spewing dust as it bounded away toward the east. Six, maybe eight Indians followed the bouncing wheels, firing as they rode. The reports followed after white puffs of smoke, sounding like firecrackers. Frightened white settlers fleeing from angry Indians. Sioux, he figured, and too many of them for one rider to make much difference. The Indians were too occupied with the buckboard to notice the tall man on the sorrel.

Gunn continued toward the low hills and pulled up next to a gnarled oak as the sun slipped behind the prairie grasses. The last glint of the setting sun bounced a reflection off an object beyond a nearby stand of trees. Gunn sucked in his breath and eased himself out of the saddle.

Voices floated toward Gunn through the underbrush.

"Lemme see them rags one more time, Whitey."

Gunn crouched low in the bushes, close enough to make out four men lounging around a small clearing.

"What do you want with a batch of bloody rags?" The man named Whitey looked rough, hard.

"Just want to look. I can't believe that lieutenant was gullible enough to believe that story about the Indian raid on those wagons."

Gunn waited, listened.

Esquire tossed his head, blew a silent snort through rubbery nostrils. He shook off sweat, rattling the

38

saddle.

"You hear something?" A third man spoke.

Gunn's heart thrummed in his chest. It was a deadly time. If he moved, Blood's men might hear him.

"I'll take a look around." The man called Whitey rose, laid his rifle across his arm and shuffled across the clearing.

Keeping pace with Whitey's movements, Gunn eased himself backward past the sorrel's rump. Grabbing the reins, he swung into the saddle, clapped spurs into the animal's flanks. The Walker cleared the brush. Gunn hunkered low over the pommel, presenting no silhouette.

Four against one at close range were not odds that Gunn favored. Open prairie and the closing darkness would even up the numbers.

Rifle bullets sizzled the air somewhere over to the right.

Gunn spurred the sorrel into a dead run away from the four men in pursuit.

Below a rise, Gunn reined in on the horse. Esquire's forefeet stabbed into the earth, sending up a spray of dust. Gunn dismounted on the run and with reins still in hand pushed hard against the horse's neck, pulled its head down toward its chest. The horse folded into the high grass. Gunn lay across his neck, pinning the animal to the ground.

The light faded as darkness came on in the wake of the sunset.

Gunn eased up, rolled the horse slightly toward him. He slipped the Winchester from its scabbard and crouched behind the horse's heaving belly. He

39

wrapped the reins around the saddle horn, rested the rifle across the cantle. Gunn patted Esquire on the neck.

"Easy. Easy, boy."

The horse lifted his head from the ground, looked wall-eyed at the kneeling man.

"Here they come, boy," Gunn muttered.

The seconds crawled.

Hoofbeats thundered toward him. A rifle boomed. A bullet whipped past Gunn's head. Whispered deadly through the grasses. High and to the right.

They had not spotted the downed horse.

The four mounted shadows loomed close. Single file, they passed within thirty yards. He let three of them go by.

Gunn led the fourth rider with the Winchester.

He levered a shell into the chamber and fired. The bullet slammed into the man's gut, knocked him from his saddle.

The other three reined in their mounts and milled in confusion.

"He got Reedy."

"You see where the shot come from?"

"Over that way," answered the one called Whitey, pointing in Gunn's direction.

The three peered into the growing darkness.

"You see anything, Joe?"

"Naw, Whitey. It's black as pitch out there. Let's fan out a little and backtrack. Keep a sharp lookout. This one is tricky."

Gunn heard the soft plod of hooves drawing closer. With patience and a still horse, the riders might pass.

Patience, hell. He was a dead man if they rode up

on him.

Gunn sheathed the Winchester. He slung his right leg over Esquire's side and grabbed the saddle horn.

"Up, boy," he whispered, jammed his left spur into the horse's tender flank. The horse rolled, lurched to its feet.

Gunn slipped into the saddle, unwrapped the reins from the horn and rammed the horse with his spurs again. The man let the horse out at full gallop, raced into the darkness away from the three hardcases.

Gunn headed toward the hills and cover. The three would likely try to run him to ground. His best bet was to split them up. Even up the odds.

Gunn led the three men into low mountains that were rugged, rocky, sparsely wooded. Skirting an outcropping of boulders, he headed across a dry creekbed and swung back to follow the gravel path. Without pausing, he searched for possible vantage points. The Walker slowed, picking its way among the river stones. The moon rose, bright as a newly minted silver dollar, dusted the land with pewter, created shadows and dark shapes.

A butte-like formation of rocks emerged out of the blackness, its silhouette frosted by moonlight. Gunn wheeled the horse out of the creekbed toward the pile of boulders. He reined Esquire in behind the rocks. He waited, watched. Listened.

The riders swung around the bend of the creekbed and came toward the waiting man. They slowed, fanned out. He let them come.

The three craned their necks. Rifle barrels glinted in the ghostly light. The lead rider pulled up. "Too much country to cover like this. I'll ride on up the wash. Whitey, you take that rock ridge over there." The man's arm gestured in Gunn's direction. "Joe, you take the other side. We'll meet back at the camp. Get that bastard. No tellin' how much he heard."

Gunn watched the three split up, one rider heading toward him. He headed the sorrel up the backside of the shelf, and cut up to a ridge of rock.

In shadow, he rode beneath the ridge. An hour passed. Gunn turned for a glance back. Nobody was in sight.

Coming to a natural break in the rock, he led the horse down the west side of the crest into an arroyo. There was thick brush, high grass for cover. He reined the horse into the underbrush and waited.

The clatter of hooves against rock floated down from the ridge.

Gunn dismounted and eased the Winchester from its sheath. He jacked a shell into the chamber, cursing the sound of metal. He propped his chest against a boulder and lifted his rifle. Nestling his cheek against the stock, he aimed in the direction of the sound.

A horse and rider trudged into view. The horse bobbed its head up and down as it picked out uncertain footing on the rocks.

The shot would have to be true to avoid the animal's moving head.

Gunn took a shallow breath, held it. His finger squeezed the trigger. The Winchester cracked. The horse screamed, went down.

The rider scrambled down the side of the ridge. Rocks clattered. The man rolled toward him, rattling the brush.

Gunn worked the lever, spun out the empty hull.

42

The action slid over the new bullet, left the hammer at full cock. He waited.

The brush moved again.

The Winchester belched an orange flame. The bullet pinged against rock.

Gunfire exploded from the bush, pinpointing Gunn's target. Bullets sizzled past his head. The Winchester cracked again. The bushes thrashed, then stopped.

Gunn jacked another shell into the chamber and fired again. There was no return fire. It grew quiet.

Gunn eased back from the boulder, reloaded in the silence. He shoved the rifle into its scabbard and mounted his horse. Keeping to the arroyo, he circled, headed back toward the creekbed.

He slowed Esquire as they approached the wash. The danger could come from either direction. He tugged on the reins, melted into the shadows of aspen trees, their trunks stark white in the moonlight.

He waited, invisible in the darkness between the trees.

The metallic click of a cocking hammer sent a shiver down Gunn's spine. He squinted steely-gray eyes, peering in the direction of the sound.

Esquire shifted under him, flicked an ear.

"That you, Joe?" a voice called from across the grove.

"Yeah," Gunn grunted the reply.

"Damn. For a minute I thought I had the sonofabitch cornered. The bastard shot my horse out from under me up there on the ridge. He thought he had me." The hardcase, afoot, began to cross into the trees toward Gunn, approaching from the left.

"Naw." Gunn grunted again. Still he did not move.

"You okay? You sound funny." The man stepped closer to the mounted figure.

Gunn smiled in the dark.

Chapter Five

Gunn slid his left hand along his thigh toward the butt of his Colt. He slipped the leather thong from the hammer. He pulled the .45 from its velvet-soft holster and rested the pistol against his belly, aimed at the approaching man.

"What the he . . ." The outlaw looked up as Gunn cocked the hammer back.

"You can empty your hands or go down," whispered Gunn.

"Fuck you," said the man, bringing up his rifle.

Gunn lined up his target, pulled the trigger. An orange blossom of flame spat from the barrel. The hardcase groaned, staggered under the sledgehammer impact of the bullet. A smear of blood began to spread where his belt buckle had been. His rifle slipped from his fingers, struck the ground with a muffled thud.

Esquire pranced sideways at the noise, flared his nostrils at the burning stench of black powder.

The wounded man fell to his knees, grabbed his belly as he knelt. Gunn cocked the Colt, approached him on horseback warily. The man's breath came hard.

"You . . . you . . ." he wheezed, the pain choking off his voice.

"All you had to do was quit," said Gunn quietly.

The man looked up, his eyes glazed frosty by the moon. He tottered, fell over. Gunn heard the terrible rattle of death in his throat. In a second or two, the man no longer breathed. Gunn eased the hammer back down, worked the ramrod. The hull shot out, clanged on stone. He slid another bullet in the empty chamber. "Damned fool," he muttered, but his gut fluttered as he thought about the useless waste of life. The dead man might have had some good years left to him. He drew a breath. It wasn't over yet. Not by a damn sight.

Gunn reined the skittish horse toward the outlaw camp.

Joe Sweet heard the gunshot in the direction of the creekbed. A single shot. "Must've got the bastard," he said to himself. There was not much conviction in his voice. Sweet circled his mount and headed for the rendezvous. He had had enough of tracking an unknown man in the dark.

There was no one in camp. "Be along soon," he said, his voice quavering. He tied his horse to a scrub oak.

Sweet crawled atop his bedding, pulled his dust-covered hat down over his eyes. He heard a scuttle in the dust near his head. He brushed his hand in the direction of the sound, hoping to scare the small

46

creature away.

Sweet's hand touched cold metal. A gun barrel.

"Don't breathe," Gunn murmured. "I'll splatter your brains all over this camp if you so much as flick an eyelash." Gunn lay on his belly, holding the .45 only inches away from the man's temple.

"What do you want, mister?" Sweet asked, the quaver in his voice more pronounced than before.

"I want Jack Blood."

"I'm not Blood. Name's Sweet. Joe Sweet."

"It's Blood I'm after," said Gunn. "You tell me where he's headed or you'll get some free land."

"The Powder."

"That's Sioux country. I thought . . ."

"Cheyenne country, too. And, Jack made a deal with Chief Old Bear."

"What kind of deal?"

"To bring Old Bear's daughter and granddaughter back. That Fanny, she's a chief kin. Green Willow Leaf is Old Bear's daughter."

"But Jack killed her," Gunn said tightly.

"Yeah, for good reason, too. It was him what made the deal to sell her off to Jacques Laurent in the first place. If Old Bear knew that, why he'd . . ."

"Sweet, you talk too much," a voice called from beyond the camp.

Gunn rolled away from Sweet into the underbrush as the air exploded with sound, filled with white smoke. The acrid stench of black powder filled his nostrils.

"Damn, Lago, what the hell? The man had a gun at my head." Sweet's voice rasped with pain.

Lago Menker laughed and fired another shot into

47

Sweet's body. Droplets of blood made patterns in the dust. From his cover in the brush, Gunn could smell the sickening smell of death.

The shots came from behind a boulder. Gunn could hear the clicks as the unseen Lago reloaded his gun. Seconds ticked by. The camp was deadly silent.

Gunn lay still, deep in the brush, in the darkness. Minutes passed. He lost track of time. Lago must be a patient man. Or long gone. Sweet, he figured, must be stone dead. It was so quiet he could hear his own heartbeat. He waited for Lago to make a move.

"Who the hell are you, stranger?" Lago broke the silence.

"The name's Gunn."

"You the one what they talk about down to Cheyenne?"

"Maybe." He tried to pinpoint where the man was at that moment. The darkness was deceptive. Sound played tricks on a man's ears.

"You killed a lot of men. Maybe you'd like to kill me."

Gunn did not reply. He started to move, crawling backward on hands and knees. He took it slow, made no sound.

Gunn heard the sound: a bootheel scraping rock. He listened hard for several seconds. Small creatures scurried in the underbrush. A far-off coyote rapped. Moments later, another made an answering call. How much time had gone by? An hour? More? He looked at the stars, saw that they had slid toward dawn. He heard a crashing sound and his heart froze in his chest. Sweat beaded up on his forehead. He kept moving, stayed low. He had circled, was now flanking the boulder where Menker had fired from ambush.

"Tell you what, Gunn. My name's Menker, out of Texas. I heard tell of you down on the Brazos, too. You shot a couple of us, but I don't fight fair. You come out and I'll blow daylight through you. You follow me, I'll put out your lamp. You savvy that?"

Gunn said nothing. Menker wasn't behind the boulder any more. He had moved too, so quietly Gunn hadn't heard him. He was downslope now, fifty yards, maybe a hundred yards away.

Menker laughed his harsh laugh. "Come on, Gunn! Now's your chance."

Gunn stood up, started moving toward the place where Esquire was hidden. He moved on the balls of his feet, avoided the brush.

Menker laughed again. The silence filled up, pounded in his ears.

"Stay there," Gunn whispered to himself. "Just stay there a little while longer."

Esquire whickered as Gunn drew near.

Then Gunn heard them. Hoofbeats. They pounded away, fading fast.

Gunn cursed silently.

Menker was gone.

Lago Menker rode his mount hard, pushing the miles, leaving behind the night and riding on past the dawn. The weariness showed in the way his sweat-soaked shoulders sagged, in the thin tight lines around his mouth, in his bleary, dust-clogged eyes. The horse, too, could not keep up this pace.

Yet there was no time to rest. He had to catch up

with Blood and the rest of the men. Another half-day's ride would bring him to the crossing of the Cheyenne-Black Hills Stage Road and the North Platte River.

Menker looked toward the far hills and saw the first puff of smoke.

Then another. Thick billows, almost like clouds.

Smoke signals. They broke up and floated like spider webs in the cloudless sky.

His eyes swept the horizon. More smoke appeared.

An involuntary shiver tingled down his spine.

He was not a coward. Just smart enough to know that a lone man wouldn't stand a chance against the angry Indians in these hills.

The man pushed his mount on toward the Laramie Mountains.

Smoke signals continued to dot the sky as the sun sank behind the distant peaks. He rode slower now, letting the horse wind. His butt burned from being too long in the saddle. He had been riding for more than a day. Seemed like a month. His nerves were rubbed raw, his belly growled with hunger. And he kept looking over his shoulder. He had bluffed Gunn out once, but he knew the man would be coming. He knew Gunn was back there, somewhere.

The trail dimmed under long shadows by the time Menker reached the North Platte crossing. His horse waded through the wide, shallow river, stopping to drink as the rider scanned the sloping river banks.

A campfire lit the dusk a little off to the north. It had to be white settlers or Blood and his men. Indians wouldn't camp along this much-used trail. Had to be white men.

"Hallo the camp!" Menker yelled loudly at about fifty yards out.

"That you, Lago?" A voice answered.

"Yeah, I'm coming in."

"Where's the rest of the boys?" A tall olive-skinned man rose from his place by the fire.

"All dead, Jack."

The dark man's mouth tightened. Black eyes narrowed over high-boned cheeks. "How's that, Lago?"

"Man named Gunn. Rode up on us at night. Overheard about our trip to the fort. Then he lit out. We chased him and he picked off Whitey and Reed. He had Sweet cornered. Joe shot his mouth off about you and Chief Old Bear so I had to shut Sweet's mouth for him."

The half-breed squatted down by the fire again and began to stir the coals with a stick. "This the same Gunn your boys ran into down Texas way?"

"The same. And he's about an hour behind me."

"Farley," Blood pointed his stick to a man bedded down beside him, "set yourself up out there to watch the backtrail."

"He'll kill you, Jack. I know him. I heard stories about him. He was traveling with us. He'll kill all of you." The young woman's voice broke the night air.

Blood turned his dark eyes toward the girl. Her raven hair and black eyes spoke of the same heritage as Blood. She was fifteen—maybe sixteen. A woman by Indian accounts.

The half-breed glared at the girl. He wanted to strike her, beat her, spread her legs. But Old Bear would never take him back into the tribe if Fanny were harmed. He tightened his lips and let her words pass.

The girl moved from the shadow of the trees and turned to Lago. "Is my father with Gunn? He's a Frenchie, a trapper. Wearing buckskins. Did you see him?"

Lago glanced at Blood. His eyes flickered.

Blood spoke up. "Fanny was knocked out when the drunken soldiers attacked the wagons. She don't remember nothing." Blood watched the girl closely while he directed his words at Lago.

Lago took the meaning of Blood's words. "We didn't see no one but Gunn. He must of broke off from the rest of the party."

"Jack, you must have seen my folks somewhere around the wagon. You know my mother. Didn't you see her when the fighting broke out?"

"Fanny, we chanced by when those drunks started their fracas. Folks was running everywhere. I happened to see you run out from behind a wagon. I grabbed you up and lit a shuck." Blood did not look at the girl's eyes. She was one of his own kind. She might see the lie. "Gunn's alive. You said that he was traveling with you. It stands to reason that your folks got away, too. Probably safe at the fort by now."

The girl raised a hand to her temple and massaged the skin firmly as though she were trying to rub up a memory. She had seen one of the riders that night. But it didn't seem like he was wearing a uniform. Then she had been struck from behind. When she woke up in Jack Blood's camp the next morning, all she had for memory was a headache. Something didn't fit. Her mother had told her tales of Blood and his evil ways. He stole and murdered among his own

52

people. That was not the Indian way. Thieving and killing of whites or another tribe were deeds of bravery. But not your own village. Not the way Jack Blood had done.

Fanny slipped into the shadows of the trees. Something was wrong here and she couldn't figure it out.

Her body began to shake with fear as she fought back the tears.

Gunn was coming after her.

She shivered in the darkness.

She had seen the look in Blood's eyes, in Lago's. These men were going to kill Gunn.

And there was nothing she could do about it.

Chapter Six

Farley Goodsmith loped his horse down toward the river and stopped in the shadow of an outcropping of rock. A waning moon hung low in the night sky.

The lookout wrapped the reins around his saddle horn and took out his makings, already bored with his turn at watch duty. He built a smoke and scanned the river crossing. A rider wouldn't be able to ease up on Jack Blood's camp without first splashing through the muddy Platte.

From his position across the river, Gunn saw the orange glow of the cigarette. No sound floated across the water and he saw only the one fire.

The lookout was alone.

There would be only three men and the girl at the camp. Four men now, with Lago there.

Gunn turned his horse and backtracked to a crossing around a bend and several hundred yards upstream from the waiting man. He crossed the shallow river, turned in the direction of the camp. He tied the big horse in a grove of trees near his crossing and headed toward the lookout.

A gunshot would be chancey. The others would hear and bullets would be too risky with Fanny somewhere in the camp. Gunn felt for his knife. The knife with its engraved legend on the blade: *No me saques sin razon, ni me guardes sin honor.* Do not draw me without reason, nor keep me without honor.

Gunn eased through the brush, taking his time, making little noise. The bare outline of a plan began to form in his mind. He'd get the guard first, then draw the others out of camp, away from Fanny.

He neared the clearing, stepping carefully over stones, avoiding brush. The edge of the rock bluff loomed close. Gunn kept out of sight as the guard shifted in the saddle, fumbled with his makings again and began to build another cigarette.

Scaling the boulder would be the most dangerous part for Gunn. If he made the slightest noise, all hell might break loose. He thought of Fanny over in the camp. If shooting started, she might not be able to keep out of the way. Jack Blood would go for her first, try to escape with her. She was his ticket back to Old Bear.

Gunn got a toe hold onto the backside of the boulder. He could hear the guard's horse stamp its feet below. Leather creaked as the rider changed position in the saddle. Gunn paused, wondering if the horse had smelled him. After a moment he slid his body up the side of the rock and onto its top like a lizard seeking a spot of sun.

He pulled his body onto the rock and squatted, poised to spring. His hand gripped the knife. It was a Bowie-type, sharp on both edges, deadly.

The guard's horse shifted its weight, uneasy.

Gunn sprang forward, throwing the full weight of his body into the lookout's side. Goodsmith hit the ground with an "ooof" as the air left his chest. He broke Gunn's fall, and the tall man pinned him as he bracketed his frame with his legs.

Goodsmith sucked in a breath, thrust his hips up to unseat his attacker. He rolled, and Gunn stabbed empty air. The downed man drew his pistol, cocked it. Gunn kicked the man's wrist, sent the pistol flying from Goodsmith's grip. The outlaw drew a blade from his boot, lunged at Gunn.

Gunn crabbed sideways, threw a hard left into the killer's side. Goodsmith cursed as one of his ribs snapped. He went down, and Gunn flung himself atop the injured man.

"Drop it," panted Gunn, as Goodsmith brought his knife up.

Goodsmith's eyes narrowed and he plunged the knife down toward Gunn's shoulder.

Gunn used his free hand to slam the man's chin upward. The knife, fingers tight around the antler handle, streaked through the air, sliced skin, veins, muscle.

A fountain of blood spurted from Goodsmith's throat, gushing over Gunn's hand. His fingers loosened and the knife fell across Gunn's back, slid to the ground. It was close, Gunn thought. He heaved a sigh, sank his own blade into the ground to wipe off the blood. He finished wiping the blade on his trousers, slid it back in its sheath.

Gunn grasped the man's belt and pulled the corpse into an upright position. Struggling under the dead weight, Gunn threw the man across the saddle. The horse shied, its rubbery nostrils quivering as it sniffed death.

Gunn patted the horse's rump as he rounded to the opposite side and drew one of Goodsmith's legs across and seated the boot in the stirrup. Using the dead man's lariat, Gunn tied first one leg and then the other tight against the fenders. He hitched the rope around the corpse's blood-soaked belly and tied a final loop over the pommel.

Gunn stepped to the animal's head, patted its neck, then turned the horse toward the campfire. He led the creature with its heavy load to within fifty yards of the grove. Gunn slapped the mount gently on the rump, backed into the darkness.

He wasted no time. He skirted the camp and found a high bluff that would afford a view of the campfire. He watched as the horse and its grisly cargo ambled into the clearing.

"Goddamn, it's Farley." Lago jumped to his feet and reached for the man in the saddle. He tried to pull the man down, but his hand turned slippery with blood. He drew it away in disgust.

"That sonuvabitch, Gunn, tied Farley to the saddle." Lago looked from his bloody hands to Farley Goodsmith's body. Farley clung to the horse's side, sticking out at an angle like a flag on a windy day.

"Cut him down." Blood came around to stand

beside Lago.

The two men struggled to loosen the rope and lower their dead companion to the ground. The campfire flickered across the blood-stained corpse.

"Jesus," muttered Lago, "that bastard cut Farley from ear to ear."

There was admiration in his voice, and fear as well.

"Pretty damned funny, Lago," said Blood. "Never thought anyone would get Farley with a knife."

"Yeah. He was the best there was—with blade or gun." Lago pulled aside Farley's boot-top. The concealed knife was not there.

He looked up at Blood, his face chalk-white.

"Christ," he whispered. "That damned Gunn not only killed Farley, but he did it up close. Face to face."

Blood's hand dropped to his pistol butt as his eyes clenched almost shut.

"I want him, Lago," he said. "I want him bad."

Voices floated up to Gunn on the cool, night air. He saw two men strip Farley from his horse, lay him out. A third man stepped into the firelight to gaze at the dead man.

"Better kill that fire," said Blood. "He's probably watching us right now."

The men began kicking dirt onto the fire.

"Can you take on Gunn, Cain? You better start backtrackin' to where Farley was when he got killed."

The third man kicked at the dirt. "Damn, Jack, he's done got Reedy, Whitey and Goodsmith. And I don't know that any one of them even got a good aim at him. I ain't no gunfighter. I ride with you and fight and plunder with you because I ain't got nothing else to do, nowhere else to go. I ain't no coward, but I don't reckon I'm no fool neither."

"What about you, Lago?" Blood, the tallest among them, looked at his companion. Gunn looked at the man who had spoken, saw his silhouette as the last of the flames flickered out. The man called Jack Blood was mostly Indian, bronze with black hair that fell straight to his shoulders. He had high cheek bones and black eyes, mean black eyes. "Can you take Gunn?"

"Hell, any man can be got. But this one's slippery as a brook trout in a deep pool."

"He got you buffaloed?"

"I was out there on that prairie, Jack, when there was four of us after him. He appeared out of nowhere and got Reedy. One shot took Whitey. Now here's Farley with his gullet slit. It'll take more than the three of us dragging a girl to take him."

Blood nodded in agreement.

"Tell you what, Jack," Lago continued. "Let him come up to the Powder. You swap the girl and make your deal, then let them Cheyenne lift his hair."

A flicker of a smile danced on the half-breed's lips.

The girl sat in the shadows, watched and listened. Her Cheyenne mother had taught her to see and hear all things around her. Her stomach had rolled into a knot at the sight of the bloody corpse. Her mistrust had grown with the words she had heard from Blood. But her heart had pounded with joy as she saw the movement on the rocks above the camp. In the dim moonlight she could see the outline of a man lying

60

flat on the granite shelf. Gunn.

The attempt to draw the three hardcases out of the camp and away from Fanny had not worked. Gunn heard the words about the Powder and the Cheyenne. Fanny was part of a deal for the old chief. It was likely that Blood would not harm Fanny, at least not until she was back among the Cheyenne.

Gunn slithered down from his rock lookout and backtracked to his horse. Wending his way upstream, he found a protected gulch, tethered the horse and bedded down for the night.

There was no way to take them if they stayed bunched up like that. If he picked one off, the other two would be on top of him. Worse, Blood would go straight for the girl. He couldn't play with her life that way. He lay on his bedroll, counted stars while he worked it all out in his mind. Fanny might be safer with Old Bear. He could not prevent Blood from taking her there now, but he would pay for what he had done. So would the others. Maybe it was better this way. Pick them off, one by one.

In the morning, Esquire moved out, fresh and eager. This was lonely country with the Laramie Mountains to the southwest and ridges leading to the Powder on the north. It was rugged country, split by canyons. Gunn swung wide of the Platte toward a ridge that followed the trail but lay half a mile away from it.

The only sounds were the horse's hooves scraping ground and the creak of saddle leather. The ridges stood out sharp against the dawn sky and the black

61

shadows of brush turned green in the early light.

Gunn kept the rocky face of the ridges to his back. Against the granite background, a lone rider would be hard to spot. He kept an eye toward the east and the trail. Blood and his men would soon be coming along, making better time than he on that worn road called the Bozeman Trail.

The lone man kept to the ridges, parallel to the trail. Soon the Platte curled around the Laramie range and headed straight west. The Bozeman swung toward the north aiming at the eastern ridge of the Bighorn Mountains and the Powder River.

The Indian outrider watched the plume of dust rise along the trail below him. He reined his horse down the backside of the mountain to a spot beneath the skyline. Here he raised his rifle and made two slow, sweeping arcs in the air.

A young brave watching the sheer mountain face turned toward the largest tipi in the village.

"Spotted Horse tells of riders approaching the village. They are not soldiers." The young man spoke to a figure seated on a buffalo skin in front of the tent. The old man did not move from his place. Black eyes peered from deep in his bronze, leathery face. Two braids showing much white hair framed the head of the old chief.

"Tell the young men to be watchful. Our summer village is not known to all who travel the white man's trail." The chief stood as the four riders entered the village.

"My heart is glad to look upon the face of Chief

Old Bear." Jack Blood spoke as he dismounted before the old man.

"Jack Blood counted coup against friends and was turned from my village. Why is he among us now?" the old man asked.

"I have brought a gift for Chief Old Bear." Jack turned toward Fanny and motioned for her to get down from her horse.

"Chief Old Bear does not need another wife." The old Indian searched the face of Jack Blood for sign.

"Look at her, Chief. Can you see the eyes of Green Willow Leaf and the mouth of your wife, Singing Bird, in her face?" Jack nudged Fanny toward the chief. "This here is your granddaughter, Fanny. Green Willow Leaf's daughter."

The chief squinted his dimming eyes and reached forward to cup the girl's chin in his hand. Fanny cringed involuntarily. Before she could realize her bad manners, she drew away before the bronze hand reached her.

"Do not be afraid, my child. If you are the daughter of Green Willow Leaf, no harm will come to you. Tell me your father's name."

The girl mustered up a small voice and said, "My father is Jacques Laurent and my mother is the Cheyenne woman, Green Willow Leaf, daughter of Old Bear and Singing Bird. My grandfather, Chief Old Bear, counted coup on many enemy, twelve on one day at Yellow Wash."

"Ha!" the old man snorted, a twinkle in his eyes. "That is a story I told Green Willow Leaf as a child. When I was a small boy in my father's village, we would chase animals and count coup on them. One day we chased some buffalo calves into a draw and counted coup on them until the sun set. You are my granddaughter. Only your mother knew that story."

"You are a good man, Jack Blood. You have brought my granddaughter to me. But where is her mother?"

"Laurent's wagons were attacked by soldiers. I managed to pull Fanny out of the fracas before she got hurt. I reckon the rest of the train made it to Fort Phil Kearny."

The chief nodded. "Tonight we will make a great feast and dance to the return of my granddaughter. Tomorrow we will kill many soldiers. Count coup on our enemy. You will help us, Jack Blood. You will show us how to fight the white man." The old man raised his arms to summon the village. "Welcome Jack Blood and his men to your tipis. They are good men. They have returned the daughter of Green Willow Leaf to our village."

From his perch above the valley floor, Spotted Horse watched the activity in the village. He did not see the plume of dust as the lone rider approached the wall of the mountain.

Chapter Seven

"Come on, gal. I ain't gonna hurt you." Lago Menker grasped both the Indian girl's wrists in one of his big hands. The man's breath blew the stink of whiskey into her face.

"What's your name, darlin'?" Lago clamped his free arm around the girl's shoulders and headed her away from the firelight of the village.

"Dancing Star," she replied, scanning the edge of the village with frightened feral eyes. Most of the men at her camp were inside the chief's tent, laughing, drunk. A woman's scream would get scant attention.

Lago continued to pull the girl into the pines that edged the creek. "Me and you're gonna have some fun, Dancin' Star." The man's words were slurred and his feet stumbled, but his tight grip on the girl's shoulders held.

When he was far enough from the village, Lago flung the girl down into the soft pine needles. His weight was upon her before she could roll out of his way.

Dancing Star squirmed as the stink of the white

man and his whiskey reeked down into her face. Lago's unshaven chin scraped the girl's face and neck as he tried to kiss her sensuous lips. "Hold still, woman. I'm just trying to do what you heathens are used to. You little squaws will roll with anything that'll have you."

Menker pinned the girl to the ground, his thick forearm pressed against her upper chest. He raised himself partly off the ground, went to his knees. His free hand worked at the buttons of his trousers, then slipped under the girl's buckskin dress, lifting it above her knees. She began to kick at him, trying to raise a knee into his groin.

Struggling with the dress, Menker was able to raise the garment above the woman's waist. Her bronze pelvis with its shimmering thatch of fine hair shone in the pale moonlight.

Dancing Star grew still. The crunch of a foot on the needle floor had quieted her squirming.

Lago licked his lips at the sight of the girl's body and reached into his pants to remove his hardened shaft. He had been too intent on his struggle to hear the sounds behind him.

A large hand reached from behind Lago and gripped the would-be rapist's chin, jerking his head upward. A sharp knife drawn below Menker's jawline left a thin track of blood in its wake. Not a deep track. Not enough to nick the jugular vein.

"Remember Farley Goodsmith, Lago?" asked Gunn, pulling the man from atop the young woman.

Dancing Star stared into the dark sockets of the tall white man's eyes. She flashed a weak smile of appreciation at the stranger. "Dancing Star, daughter of

Chief Old Bear, is grateful to the tall man for his help."

"You're Old Bear's daughter?" Gunn asked.

"Yes, I am youngest daughter of Old Bear and Singing Bird."

"Then maybe you'll recognize this." Gunn reached into his shirt pocket and withdrew Green Willow Leaf's beaded necklace, the token given him by the dying Laurent.

The girl's eyes grew large when she saw the blood-crusted ornament.

Gunn whirled Lago around, keeping the knife point against the hardcase's throat. "Who killed Green Willow Leaf, Menker?"

Lago glared at Gunn.

The tall man twisted the tip of the blade deeper into the man's hide. A fresh trickle of blood oozed down the sharp edge, across the words on the blade.

"I asked you, who killed her?"

Fear flashed in Lago's eyes. He began to tremble as the still-exposed, hank of meat between his legs went limp and began to dribble urine down his leg.

"Jack kilt her. I swear."

Dancing Star leaped to her feet and grabbed the knife from Gunn's hand. In one swift move, she thrust the blade deep into Lago's throat. Blood gushed over the girl's hand. Lago gurgled a small sound and fell back, mortally wounded. The frost of death glazed the renegade's eyes.

Staring at the bloody blade for a moment, the girl fixed her eyes in a stark gaze on Gunn's face. Without a sound, she grabbed the beaded necklace from Gunn's hand and laid the bloodstained knife in his palm. She turned and disappeared into the pines, running away from her rescuer.

"Dancing Star!" Gunn called after the fleeing girl. He followed her for a brief moment until the buckskin dress could no longer be seen in the moonlight. The darkness swallowed up Lago Menker's killer.

Gunn stood there for a moment, thinking. Dancing Star had the only piece of evidence that would connect Jack Blood to Green Willow Leaf's death. And a witness to the murder lay among the pine boughs with his throat slit by the same person who had heard the man's statement.

Gunn bent down to clean the bloody knife when the sound of moccasins pounding across the earth jolted him upright. Before he could move, the pine grove filled with Cheyenne braves.

An Indian with a torch stepped toward the cornered man. Amber light danced across the silver, blood-stained blade.

"He knifed Lago. You're a dead man, Gunn." Before the captured man could speak, Jack Blood raised his rifle butt and smashed the wooden stock into Gunn's right temple. Lights danced in the sudden blackness of his brain.

Gunn felt blackness grow deeper, blot out the dancing lights.

The tall man dropped to his knees, still clutching the knife, then pitched forward like a felled tree.

A few of the drunken Cheyenne braves whooped in delight at seeing the tall man pitch into the pine straw. Some of the younger men rushed forward to strip Gunn of his belongings.

"Hold it!" Jack Blood shouted above the melee.

"He's mine. He has killed many of my men." Blood raised the rifle barrel even with the back of Gunn's head.

"No!" The shout pierced the stillness as Dancing Star stepped into the torchlight. "This man knows things that must be heard by our chief. I have been to my father's tipi. He sleeps from the white man's whiskey. Only Chief Old Bear can mark the stick for a man in our camp."

The Cheyenne surrounding the unconscious man murmured their agreement. Chief Old Bear would be angry with those who set aside his authority.

"Bring him to the village and bind him. We will wait for the dawn and Old Bear's words."

It was a struggle for four of the younger, more sober warriors to move the tall, muscular man. They were panting with the effort as they dumped the bound man before Old Bear's tipi.

Gunn awoke to a throbbing pain in the muscles of his arms and shoulders. His arms stretched taut away from the sides of his body. His head hung forward. Heavy lids opened in the early morning sun. He saw dusty ground, scattered with pine needles. A slight turn of his head sent sparks flying before his eyeballs. His skull pounded as he tried to focus on his feet, spread far apart and tied with leather thongs about the ankles. His aching eyes strained as his gaze followed the length of rawhide to where it met and encircled a stout pole. Gunn closed his eyes and tried to remember the circumstances which led him to this predicament.

* * *

Red Arrow watched the gray-eyed white man. Guarding the prisoner was an honor for the young man. If he proved worthy, Red Arrow would be allowed to fight the next battle against the pony soldiers. The boy had wanted to go today when the runners had come into the camp telling of nearby soldiers. But the chief had stopped him. Chief Old Bear said that a young man of courage was needed to watch such a worthy enemy.

Red Arrow daydreamed of counting coup in battle as he drew in the dirt with a bone-handled Bowie knife. Flecks of blood were still lodged deep in the words on the blade.

Gunn roused at the crackle of a dry stick behind him. Dancing Star's voice floated softly through the fog in his aching head.

"Do not move, Gunn. Just listen to my words. The men of my village are fighting soldiers in the Valley of the Long Grass near to us where the sun sets. There is not much time before they will return. Red Arrow is not your only guard. The white man, Loomis, watches from the trees beyond the creek."

Gunn shook his head slightly trying to grasp the girl's meaning. His brains felt loose inside his pounding head.

"If you understand me, move your fingers. Then I will know that you hear me."

Pain shot through numbed fists as Gunn made an effort to curl his fingers. The leather thongs bit deep into his raw, bloody wrists. The slight movement of the prisoner's hands brought a sigh of relief from the concealed girl.

"Good. Now hear me. Red Arrow is bored with his

duty and does not watch closely. I will cut your bindings enough to loosen them, but they will still cling to the poles. You must gather strength to free yourself when the time comes. The daughter of my sister will see to the white man and I will make sport with Red Arrow."

This was the same girl who had thrown Gunn to the wolves the night before. He had to trust her now. He didn't have many choices.

Gunn winced in pain as he felt a tug against the strips that bound his right hand. The girl set about her work and continued to speak softly.

"Your horse is tied where you left him. You must watch my movements with Red Arrow. When my body blocks his view of you, break the weakened thongs. Move quickly. I will come to you at the horses." Dancing Star completed her task in silence as Gunn blinked rapidly, tried to clear his head.

He caught the girl's movement out of his left eye. His gaze followed her as she circled a tipi and sauntered up to the young brave on guard.

"Red Arrow is a man now," the Indian girl said. "He has been chosen to watch the killer of many whites."

The boy stood and swelled his chest at Dancing Star's words. Sunlight sparkled across the knife in the boy's hand.

"That is the enemy's blade?"

The boy nodded, pleased at the attention from the chief's daughter.

"I will trade my flint blade for that of the enemy." Dancing Star watched the boy's face as she spoke. His black eyes grew wide with indecision.

"I cannot trade," he replied.

"Look at my face, Red Arrow. Read my eyes." The girl lowered her lids seductively and moved to block the guard's view of the prisoner. "The daughter of the chief seeks a husband. A young, brave man. Trade knives with me. Then tonight when the moon rises, come to my tent to return my knife." The girl brought her hand gently to her breast and stroked downward, resting the hand on her rounded hip. The brave's eyes clouded with the thoughts of mounting the beautiful squaw. He did not hear the soft snap of leather nor the quick steps of boots upon pine straw.

"I will be alone in my tipi when the moon is above the trees, Red Arrow. I will trade for my knife then." The girl swiftly grasped the bone-handled blade and placed her flint one in the young man's hand. A flicker of a smile crossed her full lips as she turned and sashayed away from the youth. His eyes followed her swaying hips until she disappeared behind a nearby tent.

The poles behind the youth were empty. Drooping rawhide straps attested to the tall man's escape.

The young brave's eyes slitted in anger. He flushed with shame. He looked at the flint knife in his hand and threw it to the ground as if it had suddenly turned hot.

Fanny Laurent wondered how she could get away as long as Loomis was standing there. She racked her brain for a way to distract him. She said a silent prayer more to quell her fear than with any expectation that it would be answered. The next moment, to her surprise, Loomis forgot about her. In his position at the edge of the village, he had been the first to hear it.

The sound of hoofbeats, the blare of a bugle.

Chapter Eight

The creak of saddle leather and the muffled crunch of horses' hooves on the thick layer of dead, brown pine needles intruded upon the stillness of the mountains. The wind whispered through pine branches. A raccoon stopped its search for grubs long enough to watch the tall white man on the sorrel and the Indian girl on the paint pass by.

Gunn and the girl made steady progress upward into the rocky mountains, the man checking the backtrail frequently for signs of followers.

The pair rode on, winding their way toward timberline and a distant pass. Emerging from a narrow game trail into a small, sloping meadow, the two stopped to rest their mounts.

The girl finally spoke. "Old Bear and his braves will not follow us now."

"How's that?" Gunn replied, as he dismounted. He reached down, grabbed a handful of dry pine needles. He rubbed the animal's neck and chest, soaking up the sweat.

"When the horse soldiers are gone, my people will

pack their belongings and ride to another summer camp far from this place." The girl's dark eyes watched the man as he finished wiping Esquire's rump.

The two did not speak again while they munched jerky and passed the canteen between them. The wilderness around them spoke in whispering pines, scampering rodents, calling birds. The two rested, listened, then continued the journey toward the falling afternoon sun, picking their way along the animal trails and rock outcroppings.

The sun sank behind the mountain's bare peak as the pair reached timberline. Gunn dismounted and ground tied the sorrel. Here, the land was barren, stark, wild and desolate. Here a man could see a long way, feel the power and majesty of the earth where the air was thin and a man's head clear as the high lakes hidden in steep ancient craters. Gunn drew in a breath, felt its sharpness in his lungs. Here, at 10,000 feet, the light was intense, and a small sound carried a long way. Below, the pine-studded slopes seemed to go on forever.

"We'll stop here where there's wood. It gets mighty cold up this high after sunset." The wind was already blowing raw off the mountains.

They ate cold hardtack and jerky from Gunn's saddlebags, made no fire. Gunn felt that he was part of the mountains now, part of its silence, its secrets. It was very quiet, and he felt at peace. It seemed as if they were the only things alive, that they were the only human beings on earth. And though they would need game, he did not want to spoil it. Fresh meat would call for rifle fire, a noise that would echo across the hills and arouse trackers from miles around.

The man and the girl sat in the long shadows, watching the dying embers of the sun.

"Dancing Star, I'm grateful for your help back there in the village."

"And I . . . I give thanks to you, Gunn, for saving me from the . . . animal, Lago." The girl replied haltingly, shivering in the night air.

"Well, I guess that makes us even." The man stood up, cut pine boughs with his knife. He laid them out, criss-crossing them, so that they made a springy bed and began to rake pine straw into a heap with his foot. When he was satisfied that the pile of brown needles were enough for a pillow, Gunn spread his bedroll over the mattress of pine boughs, the crude pillow of straw.

"It'll be a little prickly, but at least we can stay warm, if you've no objection."

The girl nodded her acceptance of the snug bedding and crawled under the blanket. Gunn watched the light fade in the sky. Soon he heard her steady breathing, knew she was asleep. He felt the tiredness in his flesh, the weariness in his bones. He listened to the silence of evening for a long time, wondering if he could make good on his promise to a dying man. Blood was in thick with the Indians. The only ace he held was Dancing Star.

Gunn eased himself into the straw beside the girl. The pine boughs made a soft, cozy bed, as good as any boarding house. Heavy lids drooped over the steel-gray eyes. His arms still ached from the ordeal in the Indian village. He settled himself into the bedding, felt the warmth of her body on his back.

The girl stirred, pressed her breasts into his back and fitted her body against his. Gunn opened his eyes, but made no movement. The girl was tossing in her sleep. A few seconds passed. Gunn felt a light flutter as small hands began to caress his shoulders, his neck.

He turned to her. She looked into his face, moonlight dancing in her eyes.

"Do you know what you're doing, Dancing Star?" he husked.

"I know," she said. "Since I saw you last night in the clearing by the village, I have known."

Gunn sucked in his breath and twined his arms around the waiting woman, drew her close. He leaned over, brushed his lips across hers. A spark of electricity raced through his body. Her arms came up around his neck. He drew her close, kissed her again.

Flames of desire burned his lips as Dancing Star's soft breasts merged into his chest. He slid his tongue into her mouth. His loins steamed with his need. His stalk hardened, pushed against the crotch of his denims, against the girl.

She broke the kiss, drew back from him.

She lowered her head into his chest and began to tremble.

"I am sorry, Gunn. I thought of Lago . . . the pain. The white man takes by force that which is not his. I have heard bad stories, and this man hurt me much."

"All white men are not like that." He touched her cheek with his hand. It was a light touch, gentle.

"Lago hurt you," he said, as she trembled against him. He felt the nubbins of her breasts harden against his chest. He lifted her chin and kissed her softly, deeply.

"My heart soars when you kiss me. It is a good feeling. I want to be with you . . . to be your woman for tonight."

Without hesitation, the girl sat up in the cold, night air and shucked her buckskin dress.

The moonlight shimmered across her smooth, golden body.

He pulled her back down under the blanket. As he did so, she leaned over, kissed him. Her lips were full, eager. He crushed her to him. This time, her tongue slid into his mouth, encircling and caressing his moist lips. The charge of electricity surged through his being.

"Mount me, Gunn. Together we will soar above the mountain peaks." Her hand edged toward his belt. Through the cloth, she grasped his swollen manhood, squeezed it.

He quickly slipped out of his clothing, moving against the cold air and his wrought up passion.

Before pulling the blanket across their bodies, he gazed at her bronze skin. The moonlight glowed upon her firm, upthrust breasts. Her nipples tautened with desire.

He touched her, leaned down and kissed each breast, licking, teasing each nipple with his tongue. She quivered with pleasure.

Dancing Star reached for the tall, lean man and grasped the hunk of flesh growing out of his loins. She caressed him lightly, gently. Building a fire of desire between them. The fire engulfed their bodies as they came together, locked in need.

"Let us ride to the mountain's peak," she breathed.

"I am anxious for the trip to the heights where the spirits live."

He bent his neck, mouthed one of her breasts. Her back arched, and she let out a low moan of pleasure. He suckled her nipple until she withdrew.

"It hurts," she whispered, "but it is good. It burns deep inside me like a small fire."

She touched his cock, squeezed it tightly in her sweating palm. Gunn winced with the sweet pleasure of it. Then, suddenly, she dove for his loins, drew his manhood into her mouth. She began sucking on him, drawing his throbbing organ into the moist warm cave of her mouth. His veins pulsed as her lips swabbed them. Shoots of desire coursed through his penis as she drew him deeper down her throat. Her lips caved in with the force of her suction and her tongue found the tiny slit-hole and probed it until he felt the same sharp pain as she had experienced when he fed at her nipple.

She moved over him, straddling his face with her thighs. Gunn grasped her buttocks and drew her pubic triangle down to his mouth. He shot a tongue through her slick, velvet portal, felt her twitch. His tongue-tip found the love-button and laved it until she spasmed with a sudden orgasm. Her panting breath blew hot against his throbbing cock.

Again and again, she shuddered, and drew her mouth up and down his swollen stalk until he knew he could stand it no more. He pushed her away, rolled over, breaking contact.

She sighed deeply.

"Yes," she whispered, "put your knife in me."

He clasped her to him, then rose above her. Her

legs sprawled wide as she brought her hips up to meet him. He eased his throbbing stalk into her. Burrowed through the smooth tunnel, waited to strike the gate of her maidenhead. She made a sound in her throat. He pulled back, stabbing again into her sheath. There was no maidenhead.

"I am a woman, Gunn. The daughter of the chief chooses who will ride with the spirits. There are few. Take me with you to the clouds."

He plunged his stalk deep into her flesh.

The girl moaned, then sighed. The heat of her womanhood boiled over as she quivered with sudden orgasm.

Her musk rose into his nostrils as she pulled him closer, her hands splayed across his back.

He hunkered down and rammed deeper, as her hips rose to meet his. He held there for a moment, deep in the valley of the woman. She shuddered, screamed with painful joy.

He plunged in and out of her tunnel breaking the dam of her passion. Her loins gripped him tight, her hips rose with each jolt, taking him to the depths of her fruit.

"I fly like the hawk," she whispered, "like the eagle." Her moans grew deeper as wave after wave, climax after climax rocked her body.

He burned into her again and again, giving her all of himself. Stroking faster and faster, he began to feel his seed boil then burst from him in an explosion of rapture.

He fell away from her drained, yet full.

"I'm glad it was you," she whispered, her lips touching his ear.

"Hmm?"

"It could have been the animal, Lago. But it was not. It was you."

"Don't think about what might have been, Dancing Star. Think about what is."

"The spirits are happy. My heart is glad."

"My heart is glad, too," he replied, pulling her close. He kissed her again, tenderly, gently. He could taste himself in her mouth. He nuzzled her neck and in a few minutes, took her again.

She was pleased.

Together, they had flown to the eagle's heights, and beyond.

The sky was covered with a lead-gray blanket and the morning air was cold. The sun did not appear out of the foggy white light.

Dancing Star disappeared into the thicket below timberline while Gunn prepared the horses for the day's trek.

When she returned from her toilet, he was just finishing up.

"You have any idea what Old Bear's planning to do with Fanny?" The man tightened the cinch and waited for the horse to inhale before pulling it one last time.

"My sister's daughter is a Cheyenne and the granddaughter of a chief. No harm will come to her by the hand of the Cheyenne. She will be safe in the summer village."

"Where is this village?"

"It is past the creek of salt and in the valleys of the Powder River." The girl brushed her hair with a delicate hand. "Why do you need to know these things?"

"We need to get down out of these hills and head that way. You need to get back to your people and I need to be sure Jack Blood won't have a chance to harm Fanny." Gunn looked skyward. "And besides, this weather is liable to change fast. A summer snowstorm can take place any time at these heights."

The girl dumped the remains of the coffee on the dying fire. "I have been to the camp many summers. I will lead you there and speak with my father about Jack Blood."

Clouds scudded in low, thickened in the high air.

The Indian girl on the paint led the way across the barren mountain peak, through a pass wide enough for one horse and around steep drop-offs that took Gunn's breath away when he looked over the side.

The temperature began to fall as the two riders began their descent of the western slope of the Laramie Mountains.

One or two snowflakes fluttered unnoticed against the green of the pines.

Chapter Nine

The wind rose, turning the few snowflakes that dusted their faces and stuck in their eyebrows into a full blown storm.

The paint plodded on, head down, into the piercing blast. The sorrel followed, breathing hard in the thin mountain air. The Indian girl in the mackinaw pulled up, waiting for Gunn to come alongside.

"The track ahead is known to me. It is not marked. My people use this way sometimes to travel unseen to summer hunting grounds." The girl shouted to be heard above the piercing howl of the wind.

The man nodded, pulled the collar of his sheepskin coat close around his neck, then reined his mount in behind the paint. The two riders moved their horses slowly into the driving, knife-sharp wind. Snow swirled about the riders, sometimes closing off their vision past the lead horse, sometimes opening the path when a sudden gust of wind tore through the white fabric of snowfall. The girl knew the way, never stopping. She urged the paint ahead, always sure of the trail.

The blowing fury slackened as the pair descended the west side of the mountain, the horses picking up speed down the grade. The trail widened in places and wound over the easiest footing. The path was mostly rock ledge, leaving little sign from the movement of even a whole village of people. Finally, the trail opened into a small, sloping meadow.

The Indian girl drew her horse up abruptly, gazing at a structure of poles dusted white by the waning flurries.

Each bier was made of four stout saplings with a platform of pine boughs.

Esquire coned up twitching ears and whinnied nervously at the two bodies.

"It is Spotted Horse and Red Eagle." The girl's voice carried softly on the wind. The oversized mackinaw flapped against her arms as the girl reached skyward.

"This is a holy place," she announced. "These Cheyenne braves will hunt with the spirits for all time." Lowering her arms, she stepped the horse quietly around the edge of the clearing and resumed the trail on the other side. Gunn watched her silently. Dead Indians were sacred to their people. These two had probably been wounded in the skirmish with the soldiers and had died on the trail.

Both bodies were rigged out in full war paint. Indian weapons, a rifle and animal skulls lay beside each corpse. Gunn rose slightly in his saddle to gain a better look at the two men. Each was covered with a ceremonial blanket and had an ammunition belt and medicine bag at hand. A few bowls and household goods rested at the feet of the scaffolds. Both must have been brave warriors to be sent off with so many weapons and worldly goods for the hereafter.

The tall man did not want to offend the girl nor disturb the spirits in this burial place. He spurred the big horse gently and followed the edging route that the girl had taken.

The sky had lightened some, lifting the snow and the temperature. The air was still cold, but not so biting, so bone-chilling.

What little of the trail that had been obvious was gone now. Gunn could see no sign of tracks. He could not determine his bearings. He was lost.

The girl on the paint did not hesitate. She led the way around boulders and across a wide arroyo. The horses struggled up the ascent of the far side of the wide, overgrown wash.

They crossed a narrow stream, heard its gurgling as it coursed downhill. At the far edge of a stand of aspen, the land dropped off into a series of gullies and draws. Rough country that could swallow them up in the wink of an eye.

The day wore on, the air warming as the two continued their descent of the mountain.

They made a camp in a grove of old aspen, built a small fire. The foliage from the trees would spread the smoke. Only someone passing very close, within their view, would be able to smell the burning wood or see the flame.

There were no streams or creeks in this place, but they had crossed enough water during the day. Their canteens were full and the horses would not suffer.

* * *

It was midmorning of the next day when Gunn and Dancing Star reached the summer camp of Chief Old Bear. The village was nestled in a grassy canyon, sheltered by two towering rocky bluffs. A clear stream meandered through the settlement, winding among the tipis set on either side of the silvery water.

The village stirred with routine activities. Several women worked over the carcass of a buffalo calf, slicing thin strips of meat for winter jerky. Children scampered about the settlement, playing their make-believe war games. A scrawny pup yapped and nipped at the heels of the running youngsters. Tipis were set all down the grassy valley, each with its own cooking area. The large council tipi sat in the center of the village. Here and there young men worked at setting the last of the leather tents.

A few heads turned as the paint and sorrel passed. Gunn shifted in his saddle, but kept both hands on the pommel. He felt uneasy, perhaps because no one had greeted them or tried to stop them. It was clear that the pair was expected, probably had been watched for the last few miles.

Dancing Star pulled up before a large, decorated tipi. Old Bear stepped from behind the entrance flap as though on some sort of signal.

"My eyes shine on the face of my daughter and my heart sings at the news of her return."

The girl swung down from the paint. "I, too, am glad to see my father. I have brought the man, Gunn, to speak with you."

"I know of this man, Gunn. He has killed many men. Men who would not harm him. He has brought the soldiers to us. We have lost two mighty braves."

The old Indian looked at Gunn, still seated upon his horse. "Walk among us, Gunn. Look to the sky and the earth around you. Make peace with the spirits. Today, you will die."

"No, Father. This man has a good heart. He saved me from the white man, Lago. He has returned to see my sister's daughter, to see that she is safe from the harm of Jack Blood."

Old Bear looked at Gunn. Then at Dancing Star. "I will make a smoke in the pipe and think on these things." The chief lifted his arm in a sweeping motion.

Braves surrounded the sorrel. Jack Blood stood at the edge of the group.

"Kill him!" Blood shouted. "He has brought the soldiers to us. He is at fault for the death of Spotted Horse and Red Eagle!"

A murmur floated through the crowd of Indians. The chief again swept his arm through the air. "I am Old Bear, chief of the Cheyenne. I will think on these things." The old man gestured to a brave standing beside Gunn's horse. "Small Eagle, bind this man. We will hold council to decide if this is the day for the white man, Gunn, to die."

The brave jerked Gunn's hands from the pommel and looped a rawhide strap around the wrists. The Indian tugged on the thong, forcing the tall man to throw one leg over the horn and ease off the horse. The brave yanked the lead, causing Gunn to stumble. A few of the younger men in the crowd chuckled at the clumsy movement of the bound man.

Jack Blood moved close to Gunn, struck the bound man a glancing blow on the ribs. Gunn lashed out with his boot, catching the half-breed in the groin. An older brave guffawed at Blood's unfortunate predicament. The half-breed, realizing his error, glared menacingly at Gunn as his captors led him away.

Small Eagle led Gunn to a tall stake in the shade of a gnarled oak near the edge of the village. The Indian tied the leather strap to the top of the pole, allowing enough lead for the tall man to sit on the rocky ground with his arms extended overhead. He could slide the hitch up and down, but not over the top.

Gunn watched the people of the village for a while, measuring time by the pattern of sunlight filtering through the leaves of the old tree. The adults of the tribe ignored him, children occasionally came close enough to get a look at the prisoner.

There was no sign of Blood or Fanny, nor did he see Dancing Star. The sun burned across the sky, dropped low in the west, blinding him. He knew the old chief must be holding council for he saw that even the children were keeping quiet, adding to the hush that gripped the camp.

The sun went down and still no one came to give the prisoner food or water. His fate was still undecided. He was in limbo. A condemned man would be abused, taunted. To these Indians, Gunn was not yet a person. His life hung by a thread, a thin wisp, in the hand of an aging Cheyenne chief. Fires were lighted as the dark came on, and still no one came. Iron pots rattled, a baby cried, a mother crooned it to sleep. The aroma of food cooking wrenched Gunn's stomach, and he tried to think of other things.

The sound of rustling cloth brought Gunn's head

around. The cook fires in the village were dying, the Indians settling down for the night. The rustling sound came again.

"Gunn?"

"Yeah. Fanny, be careful. You could get in trouble talking to me."

"It's all right. Grandfather knows I'm here. I talked to him for a long time before he finally agreed to let me come and speak with you. I have some food and water for you. Can you drink tied up like that?"

"It'll be a little awkward. Can you hold the dipper for me?"

The young woman held the gourd dipper to the prisoner's lips. Gunn drank deep, a little of the liquid spilling down his shirt.

"Thanks. Could you manage to get me a mouthful of meat? My stomach's been complaining for a while."

"Here," she said, placing a wooden spoonful of buffalo stew near his chin.

The thick paste of well-cooked meat emitted a spicy scent as the hungry man scooped the food off the spoon with his lips.

The girl continued talking as she fed the man. "I had to beg my grandfather for quite a while before he would let me come. I told him all about the days that you had known my parents and hunted with my father. Chief Old Bear trusts me and has agreed to listen to my words after I have talked to you. You must tell me as much as you can remember about the wagon train fight and those men you killed along the way."

Between mouthfuls, Gunn recounted the story of

the wagon attack as closely as he could remember and of the words he overheard from Blood's men.

"What about my mother's necklace? Where is it now?"

"Dancing Star has it. She took it from me the night Lago attacked her."

"But don't you see? She can save you. If she shows them my mother's necklace, they will know that Jack Blood murdered her."

"Maybe she has reason not to show it."

Tears began to trickle down Fanny's cheeks, making silver tracks along her fine Cheyenne nose. The rising moon reflected the sadness in the girl's face.

"Dancing Star is my aunt, my mother's sister. Why would she keep the necklace a secret from Old Bear?"

Not having an answer, Gunn watched as the beautiful half-breed girl gathered the utensils and faded into the shadows of the village.

"That was a right purty sight, Gunn." Jack Blood stepped across the dappled moonlight toward the bound man. "Yessir, right purty. That little half-breed spoon-feeding you and crying and making over you."

"What do you want, Blood? The old chief know you're here?"

"You think you've got it all figured out, Gunn. Well, the old man didn't say I couldn't have a bit of sport with you." Blood drew back a boot and landed a vicious kick to Gunn's ribs.

The tall man grunted as the breed leveled another kick that brought tears to the corners of the prisoner's eyes.

Gunn threw his weight into his back and raised

both feet off the ground in time to ward off another kick. Blood, off balance, sprawled a few feet away. A dog somewhere close by barked.

Gunn called on his cramped stomach muscles to help pull his feet up under him and rise from a squatting position. This action slackened the rawhide strap enough to give Gunn some hand movement.

Using his bound fists like a sledge, Gunn met Blood as the half-breed stepped in to land another blow. The hide-bound hands landed a powerful blow to Blood's temple, causing the man to stagger backwards. By now, several braves had gathered to watch the fight.

Blood stepped in again, avoiding the kicking feet, and landed a fist in Gunn's gut. Breath whooshed out of the prisoner's lungs.

Gunn seized his momentary advantage, held the leather like a rope and swung his weight on the rawhide, bringing the full force of his feet into Blood's chest.

The half-breed hit the ground hard and after making a weak attempt to rise, lay there panting.

"Jack Blood is a brave warrior." One of the Indians watching the fight laughed at the man lying in the dirt.

"Yes," said another brave. "He fights well when his enemy is tied to the stake." The bystanders laughed and chuckled among themselves as they left the shadows of the big oak.

Jack Blood rolled over onto his back and with effort sat up and stared at the still-tied prisoner.

"I will kill you, Gunn. Before the sun sets tomorrow, I will kill you."

Gunn's gray eyes flashed, his jawline tautened.

"Tomorrow's as good a day as any to die. For either one of us."

Chapter Ten

"You, Jack Blood! Stay away from the white man prisoner or you will share his fate." Blood winced as the chief crawled toward the tent-flat. His lips curled in a sneer. Chief Old Bear stepped from his tipi into the dawn light. "Today, we make council," he told the braves gathered there at his lodge. "Take the tall man into the tipi of Spotted Horse. Unbind his hands and bring him food and water. Guard him. He was unhuman at this stake until his fate was decided. Jack Blood has made him human again by fighting. We must feed and care for the white man until the council has decided. Go! Now!" The old man turned his back on them and made his way back to the council lodge.

Two braves led Gunn into a tipi on the far edge of the village. A small fire burned in the center of the tent, the smoke rising gently toward the high opening. He had had little sleep and his eyes felt raw and ragged at the edges. His beard was rough, and he stank with the stale odor of dried sweat. His stomach rumbled from hunger. The braves closed the door flap as Gunn settled into a buffalo robe that lay on one side of the small lodge. A shadow flickered on the far side of the tent.

Dancing Star and Fanny sat as still as listening deer when the two men brought Gunn into the tent. They had watched Blood in his attack and knew the ways of Chief Old Bear. The enemy would be honored in the tent of a dead brave. They waited, knowing that Spotted Horse had the finest tipi.

Dancing Star's eyes glittered in the firelight. "Gunn," she hissed, "listen to me. There is a way Chief Old Bear will free you." With those few words, Dancing Star slipped quietly out of the lodge and murmured to the guards outside.

"Well?" Gunn rubbed his wrists, waiting for the girl to answer him.

Fanny edged close to the fire and sat across it from Gunn, her cotton skirts billowing like clouds as she seated herself. She lowered her head, hesitant to speak to the handsome man.

"Dancing Star said . . . she said . . ."

"What is it, Fanny? Cat got your tongue?" Gunn spoke gently, sensing the girl's discomfort.

"Gunn, I'm scared." The olive-skinned face became visible as she looked at the big man.

"I know, Fanny. I know. I'm in a bad spot. You too, maybe. We need to get out of here. Jack Blood won't rest until he sees both of us dead."

The girl mustered her courage. "Dancing Star said that I must sleep here . . . with you."

"Sleep here?"

"You know. Sleep with you." The girl lowered her eyes, blushed. "She said that if I sleep in the blanket with you, then my grandfather will consider us married and won't kill you. He wouldn't kill his own grandson. And that is what you would be." Fanny continued to stare into the fire.

"Dancing Star said that?"

"Yes, she said you were good, strong. Chief Old Bear would not question my choice of husbands."

Gunn moved around the small fire and squatted beside the girl. Taking her hand, he pulled her to him. Something inside her was like a frightened deer. She looked at him with a fawn's eyes, and she trembled. He had seen such looks before. There was both desire and fear in her eyes.

"Listen to me, Fanny. I've known you since you were no bigger than a gopher. I wouldn't force you into such foolishness just to save my own hide. We'll get out of this mess, but it won't be done by hiding behind your skirt. Now you go on back to your lodge and don't worry about me. I'll figure something out."

He led the girl to the tent flap and patted her hand.

"Now, go." Gunn flung back the hide covering and crawled aside to let the girl pass.

The face of a young brave poked into the tent.

"Girl stay," he said and pushed Fanny backward into the tent.

The head of another brave appeared over the shoulder of the first. "Girl stay," echoed the second brave, nodding his head.

The first Indian closed the flap on the surprised couple.

"Well, it looks like you stay here, Fanny. Our two friends out there seem to have orders to keep you in here with me."

"Yes, so it seems," she replied.

"Somebody sure wants us both alive," he said.

"Dancing Star," whispered Fanny.

"Maybe."

"No, she does. She . . . she loves you."

"Now, what makes you say that?"

"Because I know. A woman knows such things."

Her voice was very quiet, and Gunn looked at her hard as a shaft of sunlight shot through the smoke-hole. Its gauzy column shimmered with dust motes. Fanny heaved a sigh and settled back on a buffalo robe. Gunn saw the woman in her then, saw that the girl he had once known had grown up and gone away.

Jack Blood stood in the center of the council lodge, his arms raised to the gathering of the chief and his twelve advisors.

There had been much talk before this, many smokes of the pipe. It was enough to wear down a white man's patience. And Jack considered himself a white man when he was in civilization. His Indian blood was handy when he was among the tribes.

"Old Bear, Chief of the Cheyenne, mighty hunter, brave warrior, I would speak to the council."

"Speak, Jack Blood."

Blood lowered his arms and circled the council, facing each in turn. Completing the circuit, he seated himself at the foot of the circle opposite the chief.

"I am Jack Blood, child of the Cheyenne woman, Bleeding Dove. My father was a Frenchie trapper. My blood is made of the same mix as the chief's grand-daughter. Now I am back with my true people, the

Cheyenne. I will speak the truth when I tell you of the man, Gunn and the evil he has brought to the Cheyenne."

"How do you know the white eyes, Gunn?" Snow Hunter was a cautious man, wanting to know all the information before making a decision.

"I have heard of this Gunn for many seasons. He has murdered and killed across the grasslands, killed many Indians. I will tell you my story of the search for the granddaughter of Chief Old Bear and of the murderer, Gunn."

The half-breed paused to glance around the circle. All faces were turned in his direction, waiting for his tale.

"My men and I had searched for the granddaughter of Old Bear for many moons. We had stopped by Fort Phil Kearny to find that the wagon train carrying the girl had not yet reached the fort. We backtracked in time to find the group being attacked by a gang of drunken soldiers. The girl was running away from one of the bushwhackers when I grabbed her, swung her onto my horse and lit out of there. There were too many of them and only a handful of us."

Several of the council members nodded approval at Blood's decision not to engage in battle against uneven odds.

"Well, then, I headed north here with a few of my men to bring the girl to her grandfather. And four of my men turned back toward the fort to report the attack."

Again there was grunting and nodding at Blood's decision.

Blood studied the men seated before him. No

mention had been made of Green Willow Leaf's death. Blood hoped there would be none.

"Then Gunn, he came from out of nowhere and killed three of the men headed for the fort. If it hadn't been for Lago getting away, we'd 'a never known what happened to them. Then Gunn tracked us down right away. Of course, we was traveling a bit slower on account of the girl being with us. This Gunn starts trying to ambush us one by one. He slit Farley Goodsmith's throat from ear to ear. The girl seen it, too. Well, then we just lit out for here as fast as we could. Some of you saw Lago Menker. His gullet was slit just like Farley's."

The young brave, Red Arrow, spoke. "I would ask a question of this man, Chief Old Bear."

"You may speak, Red Arrow."

"Jack Blood, what is the reason that the white man, Gunn, pursues you and your men?"

"Well, best I can figure, this Gunn wants the girl for his woman. She spoke of him on the trail, even said once that he would kill us." These last few words were the only true ones that Blood had spoken to the council. But he felt confident that these men would believe a Cheyenne . . . even a half-breed.

"Many men have done foolish things for the eye of a squaw." Snow Hunter chuckled as he finished his words.

"And one more thing," Blood continued. "Gunn doesn't seem to care how many of the brave Cheyenne get killed. He brought the soldiers down on us, didn't he?"

Chief Old Bear raised his hand to silence the mutterings of the group. "Now I would have the

100

words of my advisors. Snow Hunter, begin."

Each man in turn spoke his opinion of the situation and the verdict for Gunn. Each believed Blood and wanted Gunn's death. Each . . . except for the young brave, Red Arrow, who rose and faced the chief.

"I am young, Chief Old Bear. There is much that I must learn. So I must learn from the spirits and the earth and the men who walk here. You have taught me much about the spirits and the earth, but you have told me that I must learn about the men who walk here from each man I see. You have taught me to learn from friend and enemy. Sometimes there is confusion. A man who speaks as friend has the eyes of the enemy and the man who would be enemy has the heart of a friend."

The chief nodded at the young man. "You learn well, Red Arrow. But we must speak of the white man, Gunn."

"This man, Gunn, is strong. Not just in defeating his enemy, but in his heart. I have seen him with your granddaughter and I have seen him with Dancing Star. He protects them. I do not see bad in him because he protects them. I came upon the death place of the white man, Lago Menker. Dancing Star was there and then gone. Gunn stayed and was captured and bound. I am not sure all was seen or all is known about the death of this one man."

"Enough!" Chief Old Bear interrupted. "Many of our braves found the man and the knife and the dead one. We have talked long enough."

The old man rose and wrapped his buffalo robe tighter around his body. He walked slowly to the tent flap of the council lodge and stood there for several moments. The council had been long and the sun had passed over the mountains. It was time to make his decision, but he would not speak until he had talked to the spirits, until he knew if his medicine was good. If the spirits did not talk to him, then he would need the good medicine.

This man who had led his people through war, starvation and plenty, had much to think about this night.

Red Arrow had spoken well. He was a brave young man who could lead the tribe. He was wise for his time on earth. Snow Hunter was cautious, but in agreement. The others usually followed the words of Snow Hunter and the chief. But what of Jack Blood?

This man had been a Cheyenne and left the tribe to live among the whites. Then he returned with the child of Green Willow Leaf. Her name went unspoken this night. Did Jack Blood know of Green Willow Leaf? The man, Gunn, did he know of Green Willow Leaf? Is this what Red Arrow saw in the eyes of the friend and the enemy? The man, Gunn, has killed no Indian of the Cheyenne. But he brought the enemy soldiers who killed two of the bravest of men. Someone must pay for the loss of two brave warriors. Someone must answer to the spirits for their lives.

The old man stepped through the flap, and walked toward the brush at the edge of the camp and looked to the mountains and the stars that speckled the night.

The spirits did not speak to the old man this night. His body grew weary, but his thoughts became clear as he returned to the council lodge and the fire of his advisors.

The gathering quieted as the old man entered and took his place at the head of the circle.

"I am Old Bear, Chief of the Cheyenne. This day I have mourned to the spirits for the loss of Spotted Horse and Red Eagle. These braves watch us from the place of the spirits and cry for revenge. I would stop their tears. I would give them peace. This man, Gunn, did not kill the Cheyenne. He has only killed others of his kind. For this, he will be rewarded. But the man, Gunn, brought the soldiers who killed Cheyenne. And for this, Gunn will be punished. For this, Gunn will die."

Jack Blood could barely suppress a smile. Firelight flickered across his impassive face.

Now, Gunn would die, he thought.

And with him the truth of what happened that night when the chief's daughter was murdered.

Chapter Eleven

Red Arrow walked from the council lodge toward the tent of Spotted Horse. The camp was quiet. He moved slowly, as if the message he carried was a heavy weight on his shoulders. The horses nickered, snorted in the night air. The young brave paused for a moment under a cedar. He had requested the mission, it was the least he could do for the man who had gained respect in the Indian's thoughts. Taking a deep breath, Red Arrow continued walking to the tent of the condemned man. There, he spoke softly to the two guards.

"Gunn," The brave nudged the sleeping figure and spoke softly. It had not surprised Red Arrow to find the chief's granddaughter bundled up beside the tall white man. "Gunn." The man repeated his whispered plea.

"Umm?" The white man roused from his deep sleep to blink at the young Indian outlined by the fading fire.

"Yeah?" Gunn sat up and ran his hand over his face to clear the fog of sleep from his eyes.

"We talk."

The two men moved away from the sleeping girl to the far side of the lodge. Red Arrow tossed a small pine knot into the coals to take the chill off the high mountain air.

"Talk to me, Red Arrow."

"You know my name, Gunn, and I know yours. I spoke for you at council tonight. There is something that remains unspoken. I do not know it. Only you and Jack Blood know of these things. And neither of you speak. Now you must tell Chief Old Bear of these unspoken things. I could see the evil in Jack Blood and I see the good in Gunn. Now you must tell of this."

"There isn't much to tell, Red Arrow. I cannot prove what I think, what I have heard. Just as you cannot prove what you see in a man's eyes or his heart."

"You must say these things. Say them tonight. Chief Old Bear has decided that you must die to make peace with the spirits of Spotted Horse and Red Eagle."

"Oh, no!" Fanny whispered loudly as she boiled out of the robes. She had listened to most of Red Arrow's plea. "Gunn, you must tell Chief Old Bear what you suspect."

Gunn crept across the tent and grabbed the girl by the shoulders. "Fanny, I cannot prove any of this. It's my word against Blood's. Blood is one of your people. Now settle down, we'll think this through."

Red Arrow rose, nodded to the pair and slipped through the flapped opening into the darkness.

"Oh, Gunn, what are we going to do?" The girl was

sobbing loudly now.

"Hush, hush, Fanny." The man curled one arm about the girl's shoulders.

She nestled into his chest and cried the fear and anger out of her heart.

The couple sat close for a time until the sobbing became whimpers.

"Gunn, why did you come after me, really why?"

"I promised your pa. He was dying. Must have been real important to him. He knew he didn't have much time left when he asked me to find you. He knew your mother was already dead. Jacques was a good friend. He'd have done it for me."

"Wasn't any of it because of me, Gunn?"

He let out a breath. She asked hard questions. Maybe he had come after her because he didn't want her to wind up as a slave, or worse. And he had thought of her being all alone, taken away from a chance for a better life than she would have with a band of Plains Indians. There was, however, no easy answer to her question.

"Well, sure, Fanny. We've been friends since you were a little girl. You're a young woman now. I wanted you to be safe. Maybe take you back to your pa's folks."

"But, Gunn, Red Arrow said that my grandfather would kill you tomorrow. What are you going to do?" she whispered.

"We'll worry about that tomorrow. We need to rest and be ready for whatever comes."

"Thanks for coming after me. I'm sorry everything turned out such a mess because of me."

"Don't blame yourself, girl. You just got caught in

the middle of something that was none of your doing. Now lie back down and get some rest."

The girl lay back, but her gaze held on Gunn's face. The firelight flickered in the clear depths of his steel-gray eyes.

"Gunn, lie down with me."

"Huh?"

"Lie down with me, please. This may be your last night on earth and I owe you. I owe you a lot. Please."

"Girl, you'd better get some sleep."

"I will if you stay here by me. I want to be close to you tonight. I—I want you to hold me like you used to do, when I was a little girl."

He could understand that. Sometimes he had rocked her to sleep when her mama was too tired, or tending to her father when he had drunk too much. She had been a pretty little girl, wide-eyed, and her hair soft as silk. That tawny skin, so flawless, flawless now . . .

"I feel something when I'm close to you, Gunn. Earlier tonight when I was wrapped in the robe and you lay down nearby, I could feel your warm breath. It worried me, you know, inside."

Gunn gazed at the girl. More woman than girl.

Fanny kept her dark eyes fixed on Gunn's face and stood, letting the furry wrap drop to the ground. She unbuttoned her dress-front and let the garment slip down around her feet. She stared at him boldly as she shucked the remainder of her undergarments and stood naked in the flickering firelight.

"Fanny?" Gunn tried to speak, stop the girl, but she knelt down before him and lightly brushed her full lips across his. A shiver crawled down his back-bone.

"Shhh," she whispered and continued kissing the man lightly across the lips and cheeks. "I want this, Gunn. I have for a long time. You just didn't know that I was ready for it yet."

She squirmed against him, pressing her smooth, golden body against hers. They were both kneeling now. His arms came around her, stroked her silky skin.

She ground her loins into his, felt the swelling of his cock through the denim. Her breath blew hot on his face.

"Fanny, no," he said, fighting hard to compose himself.

"You want me, Gunn. I can feel it." The woman-child reached down and firmly gripped the outline of his swelling shaft in her hand. "I want to feel you closer," she whispered.

He started to protest, changed his mind. Her free hand began to work the buttons on his trousers. It was too damned late to stop what she had started. And he had no place to run. Still it was a big step. This girl, grown into a woman, had been like family. Once. But, he wondered, were any of them the same as they once were? Her folks were dead, so was his wife. Now, here in the lodge, they were outside of time, they were different people than they once were, new people, with new discoveries to make, new terri-tories to explore.

"Fanny, are you sure you know what you're doing?"

She smiled softly, a misty, far-away look in her eyes. "Yes," she hissed. "I am sure about this. More sure than I've ever been before."

"Fanny," he rasped, "you might not like yourself much in the morning. We can stop now and no harm done."

"No!" she husked firmly. "We can't stop now. I'm burning up inside."

He knew she was right. Whoever they had been before, they were now just man and woman. He wanted her. She wanted him. And he knew there was an added spice to all this—there was danger, perhaps death for him no matter what happened between them. His temples throbbed with his pounding pulse-beat and his heart thrummed in his chest.

"Damn, Fanny, you make it hard on a man."

She giggled softly, fisted his cock until it turned to stone.

Fanny squirmed against him, fumbled with his buttons. He brushed her hand aside and finished what she had started.

The girl grabbed his swollen manhood again, squeezed it gently. The blood surged, throbbed, stiffened it more.

She slid her hand up the hardened shaft, ran her finger across the velvet of his crown. Gunn winced in pain, pleasure.

Her small, upturned breasts rubbed against the fine hair of his chest. Her nipples turned to hard nubbins with the intimate friction.

She reached up, kissed him firmly, deeply on the mouth.

He responded to her, pulled her close. His hips answered the gyrations of hers, grinding in rhythm.

Her soft, wet lips tantalized him; her tongue slithered inside his mouth, groping, plunging.

"I want you so bad, Gunn," she breathed.

"No regrets?"

"None. I've wanted to touch you for so long. You're so hard. All over." She kneaded his muscles with eager fingers. Massaged his body with hers.

He couldn't stop now, he knew.

He grabbed her shoulders firmly, pulled her down with him onto the soft fur of the robe. He kissed her hard on the mouth.

"Yes, yes," she moaned.

He kissed her taut breasts, tongued her nipples, fondled them with his mouth. She squirmed, moaned with pleasure.

Her eyes glittered in the glow of the fire. Her mouth opened, released a sigh of wonder.

"Now, Gunn, take me now," she murmured.

He spread her legs, slid between them.

He slid past the velvet lips of her womanhood, into the moist, slick tunnel. She twitched, a groan escaping from her lips. Her fingers dug into the muscles of his back. He sank deeper into the tight cavern, rammed into the leather barrier of her maidenhood.

"You're the first," she hissed. "I'm so glad it was you, Gunn. I've wanted this so long, so long."

"It might hurt some," he whispered.

"I don't care. I don't care."

She writhed, twisted her hips, ground her loins into his. He plunged into her with short, ramming strokes, pounding her maidenhead. He pushed against it with the engorged head of his shaft, stretching, tempering its rigidity.

She moaned, catching her breath with each battering stroke against her hymen. He struck again and again, feeling it give a little with each stroke, delving deeper and deeper with each thrust.

"Yes, yes," she moaned, her longings in control of her body.

The dam of her womanhood burst as his cock hurtled, thrust deep into the virgin realm of her sex. She screamed with pain, with pleasure, her hips out of control, rising to meet him with each deep, pleasurable thrust.

The robe twisted, roiled, under the flailings of the two lovers, their moans filled the close, cool air of the lodge. The coals of the fire burned low, popped and crackled as the two lovers intertwined their bodies, groped one another for possession, domination.

Fanny rose past the pain to the heights of approaching orgasm. Her senses reeled, soared with feelings she did not understand. She shuddered, murmured, "Yes, Gunn. Oh, yes."

The heat of her virginal depths enveloped, swallowed, his surging cock. She bucked with orgasm, clutching him tighter than before. Her battering loins matched the intensity of his; the sounds of smacking flesh filled the tent.

He stroked her fast, faster, sliding in and out of her hot, wet cavern until she gasped for breath, gripping his shoulders as she rode the peaks of her orgasms. Each peak rose higher than the last, shaking her violently.

He could no longer sustain her pleasure as his seed boiled at the base of his shaft. The rising tide could not be turned as he gripped her tightly, whispered in her ear.

"Now, Fanny. I'm coming now."

"Oh, yes, yes," she sobbed. Unleashing the last explosive burst within her, she rose to meet each of his final thrusts with savage fury.

His fount of seed exploded, spewed into the steamy velvet of her cunt.

Her teeth gripped into his shoulders to stifle the scream that rose in her throat.

He kissed her cheek, held her close with his final shudder, then collapsed against her, his weight crushing her body beneath his. He held her tightly for a long time, tasted the salt of her tears as they coursed silently down her radiant cheeks. She brushed his hair, wiped the rim of sweat from his forehead. Finally, after a time, he rolled from her slippery body, lay beside her, satisfied, at peace.

Chapter Twelve

Red Arrow watched the slumbering pair for a moment, hesitated to awaken them. The day would not be a good one for Gunn. A day to die. A day to breathe out his spirit, loose it from its earthly bounds. The white man's arm lay across the shoulders of the sleeping girl. She slept soundly, peacefully.

"Gunn?" The brave touched the forearm of the condemned man then gently gripped the muscular shoulder. "Gunn, it is time. You come now."

A form, a bronze face floated before the steel-gray eyes. The braid-framed face appeared through the sleep-shrouded fog.

"Red Arrow?" Gunn sat up easy so as not to disturb the girl. He rubbed his hand across his face, cleared out the sleep gravel from the corners of his eyes.

"It is time." The Indian spoke softly, held a rawhide thong looped for binding. "You come, see chief."

Gunn groped for his clothes, stood up, naked. Red Arrow looked him over, grunted his approval. Gunn dressed quickly, without shame, finally tugged on his boots.

"Tie hands," said the brave.

Gunn nodded, extended his hands. The two men looked into each other's eyes, understanding, consoling without words. "Behind," the brave uttered. "Hands behind back." Gunn complied.

Fanny was awake now, sitting up. She watched the brave slip the loop of hide over the crossed wrists at her lover's back. Fanny's face was impassive, and Gunn saw the strength there now. She did not cry, nor break down. Instead, she pulled on her dress, tossed aside the buffalo robe and smoothed her garment. Her hand brushed at her hair, then she stood and silently followed the two into the glare of the rising sun.

It took a moment for Gunn's eyes to adjust to the brightness of first full light. He blinked, then scanned the campsite. It appeared that the entire village had turned out for the proceedings. The council Indians stood silently, bunched before the chief's tent, their backs turned toward Gunn.

Somewhere a lone dog sent up a yip, breaking the silence in the still, crisp air.

Gunn always wondered how he would feel on the last day of his life. He had always hoped he could meet death when the sun was shining, when the earth was sweet and illuminated, the blue sky flocked with pure white clouds. It seemed a good time to give up his spirit, cross the boundary between life and death. And he had wanted to meet it head on, with his eyes open, not snarled in darkness, sick, maybe, or wounded. He felt strong this morning, stronger than the red men who would kill him to avenge the deaths of braves he did not know, had not killed.

Red Arrow led the bound prisoner toward the group, brushing several aside to make way. Without force, the guard led Gunn to a lone lodge pole set to the side of Chief Old Bear's tipi.

Gunn stood there as the Indian tightly wound the rawhide strap around the pole, secured it. Red Arrow felt a friendliness toward the tall white eyes, but the brave was not a traitor to his people. He pulled the binding tight. Gunn grunted at the pressure, the sudden brief pain. The ropes cut into his flesh, locked him tight to the pole.

The crowd, still silent, parted to allow the old chief into the clearing around the lodge pole. Gunn was impressed at the dignity in the man's bearing, his regal gait. He admired the Cheyenne, knew them to be an honorable people. Under different circumstances, he knew, they might have become friends. But the tribe had been hounded by the white men, pushed past the limits of human patience. Renegades like Blood did not help salve the wounds, either. Such men kept the flames of war burning, the wardrums beating.

"You are Gunn," the old man stated. "You have killed others of your kind on the land of the Cheyenne. For this, you will receive honor. You will not die the death of a coward, stretched in the sun. You have led the horse soldiers into our village. Two of our greatest warriors are dead at the hands of the blue coats. For this, you will die."

A low murmur arose from the gathering. Chief Old Bear raised his arm for silence.

"You will die with dignity at the hand of Jack

Blood."

Gunn scanned the faces of the crowd, spotted Blood standing between two braves. The half-breed wore a smirk on his face. His eyes crinkled with light, showing that he would relish the task assigned to him.

Gunn's gaze swung back to Old Bear.

"The Cheyenne chief is wise in many things," said Gunn. "He has many winters of wisdom. I, Gunn, respect my Cheyenne brothers. They are strong in war, good hunters. But Old Bear speaks of dying with dignity, yet chooses this two-faced man who is half-white to kill me. There is no dignity in such a death. Blood is a coward who hides behind his Indian father when he is with the Cheyenne, talks out of the other side of his mouth when he is with his white man brothers. Is this the man who will kill me? He is not Cheyenne. He is not white. He is without honor."

Although the chief's face betrayed no emotion, his eyes flickered with anger. The other braves seemed to draw a collective breath. Blood's face contorted in rage. He opened his mouth, but before he could say anything, the chief's attention was drawn to another.

"Grandfather, please. May I speak?" Fanny stepped from the circle to face the old man.

The chief glowered at the impertinence of the young woman. "There is too much talk. The time for talk is no more." The Indian leader turned his back on the girl, nodded to Jack Blood.

Gunn tried to warn her with his eyes. He had already stung the chief with his words. Old Bear had made his decision. He thought it was ironic that Blood and Fanny were involved in this. Both were half-breeds. One wanted him alive, the other wanted

118

him dead.

"Father! Wait!" Dancing Star burst through the circle and extended her hand, palm up, before the old man could silence her. "Look!" She indicated the necklace that lay across her outstretched fingers. "This belonged to my sister, Green Willow Leaf. Jacques Laurent gave these beads to Gunn over the body of my sister. The man gave up his spirit and sent Gunn to save the child, Fanny. The blood on this necklace is the blood of my sister, Green Willow Leaf. Speak to Jack Blood of Green Willow Leaf's death."

The eyes of the camp focused on the face of Jack Blood, a face that suddenly drained of color.

Chief Old Bear fingered the beaded necklace. "This beaded things bears blood. Is this truth, Jack Blood? Is this the blood of my daughter, Green Willow Leaf?" The old man turned, faced the half-breed.

Jack Blood stood still, glaring at the amulet in the chief's hand. Blood had no answer, no defense. Several braves moved in, closing on the guilty man. One of them took his pistol. "Dancing Star lies!" he shouted. "Gunn lies!"

The chief spoke again. "You have spoken against this white man and the council believed you. But you do not speak with straight tongue now. Where is my daughter, Green Willow Leaf now? Where is her spirit? I cannot see into your heart, but the white man with the gray eyes does not hide behind loud talk." He turned to the braves flanking the condemned prisoner. "Release the man, Gunn. Bind his hand to that of Jack Blood. Bring the knives. The spirits will decide who speaks the truth."

119

The crowd murmured its approval. The Indians milled about, speaking with excitement about the impending contest. Jack Blood nodded to Bill Loomis who stood outside the circle of Indians. Loomis approached his partner, stepping close to hear Blood's whispered words.

"First chance you get, you shoot that sonofabitch in the back." Red Arrow heard Blood's words as the young brave stepped forward and tied one end of a six-foot thong to Jack Blood's left wrist, and then looped the other end of the rawhide strip around Gunn's left wrist. The brave gave the thong a jerk, pulling it tight against the combatants' hands. Red Arrow shot a glance toward Fanny, signaling for her to watch the white man, Loomis.

Chief Old Bear held his hand aloft. "This is a fight to the death. The winner will be free to walk among my people, to go where he chooses. The loser will receive the burial of a coward. His bones will be left to bleach in the summer sun. Let the spirits choose."

Gunn nodded to Old Bear. His respect for the old chief rose. He did not back down on his decision, but he gave it up to the spirits. It might be that Jack Blood would be his executioner after all. But Gunn's blood would not be on the chief's, nor the tribe's hands. This was the honorable way. This was the Cheyenne way.

The whole tribe, children included, surrounded the pair who were poised to fight. A cry rose from the circle of Indians as Red Arrow stepped forth with two knives. Gunn recognized the antler-handled Mexican blade that had been his trusted weapon in many fights before. The sun flashed along the inscribed legend as the brave handed Gunn the familiar knife. Blood grabbed the leather wrapped handle of the other weapon, a deadly Bowie, big-bladed, both edges honed to a razor edge. Red Arrow stepped back. Old Bear signalled for the contest to commence. His arm sliced the air in a downward thrust.

The crowd sucked in a collective breath.

Jack Blood leaned his weight against the thong, then let go. Caught unaware, Gunn lost his balance for a moment, stumbled backward to the ground.

Fanny watched, her face blank but her heart lodged in her throat.

Blood held his knife aloft as he leaped toward Gunn's sprawled form. His face grimaced with a naked savagery as he lunged. The half-breed swung the blade downward, confident of his mark. The attacker paid for his carelessness as Gunn caught a leg with his boot, sending Blood to the dirt.

Gunn scrambled, brought up one knee as the half-breed spun to his feet. The white man faked a jab with the blade and rammed his bound fist into Blood's paunchy gut.

The air rushed from Blood's chest as the half-breed slashed crosswise with his knife. The reflex action caught the fabric of Gunn's shirt, leaving a fine line of blood, thin as a pencil mark, across the white man's shoulder.

Fanny watched the line of red grow, dampening the tall man's sleeve. She wanted to stop this savage display, wanted to rush in and free this man she loved. She remembered Red Arrow's unspoken warning and fixed her eyes on Loomis who stood opposite her, across the circle. To her right stood the brave with Blood's gun. Fanny began to inch toward the armed brave.

The two fighters circled warily. Jack slashed at Gunn again. The white man jumped back instinctively, jerking the half-breed off balance. The blades glistened in the sunlight as each man in turn feinted, parried. The crowd watched, silent now.

Under the pretext of watching the fight, Loomis' eyes held the struggling men in view while his hand slid downward toward his pistol. Fanny noticed the slow movement from her position beside the unwary, armed brave. His arms folded across his chest, the young Indian dangled the .44 Remington loosely from his hand.

Blood chose that moment to rush Gunn, brought his knife arcing downward. Gunn slid from under the glinting blade and jabbed with his Mexican knife. Blood oozed from Jack's side, bringing a grunt of approval from the Cheyenne.

Jack was beginning to tire and took the chance to search the crowd for Loomis' position. Gunn took advantage of the brief pause and caught Blood's throat in his free hand, flinging the half-breed off his feet. Jack recovered, brought his knife upward, slashed the knuckles of Gunn's knife-wielding hand. Gunn stepped inside the thrust and rammed his knife through Blood's shoulder muscle.

A mutter of approving grunts issued from Cheyenne throats as Blood's hand went to the wound. His palm came away sticky with blood. The half-breed caught Loomis' eye and nodded. Jack pulled hard on the thong, jerking Gunn around so that his back was now exposed to the white man with the gun.

Loomis pulled the pistol from its holster, cocked it. The barrel was aimed at Gunn's broad back. The finger crooked around the trigger.

Loomis' movements did not go unnoticed. Fanny, terrified, her hands trembling, searched the man's face for a sign of action. The barrel of Jack's gun hung a breath away, still dangling in the unsuspecting Indian's lax hand.

Jack lunged into Gunn for the kill, his blade slashing for the white man's throat. Gunn reached up, grabbed Blood's wrist, stopped the motion. Jack glared at Loomis, twisted Gunn around, pushed him toward the gunman.

With a clear shot at Gunn's back, Loomis' finger curled tightly around the trigger, squeezed.

Chapter Thirteen

Fanny saw the flicker of intent shadow Loomis' eyes. She snatched Blood's pistol from the unsuspecting brave's fist. Her hands trembled as she extended the weapon at arm's length. Cocking the trigger, she fired pointblank at the bridge of Loomis' nose. The .44 bullet blew a hole in the man's forehead, opening up his skull. The white man's brains exploded in a cloudy pink spray. Loomis pitched forward, lifeless. His muscles twitched reflexively for several moments. His sphincter muscle collapsed, filling the air with a foul stench.

The bullet from the dead man's gun skittered along the ground, burying itself under dirt.

The Indians shouted, began speaking excitedly. Some milled in confusion. A few Indians surrounded the fallen body of Bill Loomis. Others scattered away to safety. Some grabbed their own rifles.

Gunn dropped into a crouch. His instincts gripped him at the explosive sound of the gunfire. He felt a tug on the leather thong and looked up in time to see Jack Blood rip his blade across the rawhide strap.

The hide gave way under the blade and the half-breed, free, melted into the crowd.

"Gunn? Gunn? Are you all right?" Fanny sobbed, almost hysterical.

"Fine, Fanny. I'm fine." He stood up and placed his arm around the shoulders of the frightened girl. The loose end of the rawhide thong dragged a pattern through the dust. "Loomis got killed. Why?"

"When I saw you go down, I just knew you were . . . were dead. I couldn't bear it. Oh, Gunn." The girl buried her head into the man's chest and sobbed, out of control.

"Fanny, you should know by now that I've ridden enough trails and I've learned to duck whenever I hear gunfire. What happened, anyway?"

"Loomis was going to kill you. He's dead."

"Yeah. But how did you know?"

"Red Arrow heard Blood tell Loomis to kill you. Loomis drew a bead on your back and was about to shoot you down, when . . . when he got shot."

"Red Arrow's going to be in serious trouble for firing that shot. Chief Old Bear's not going to like it much."

"It wasn't Red Arrow who shot Loomis, Gunn."

"No? Then who did?"

"Me." The girl turned, ran through the pack of Indians crowding around the dead man, disappeared from sight.

Gunn tried to follow her, but was jostled by the Indians. The black hair of the girl disappeared among the shoulders of the taller braves. Gunn still strained his eyes, searching as the old chief broke through the crowd.

"Where is the half-breed, Jack Blood?"

Gunn held up the loose binding that dangled like a leash from his left wrist. "Gone," replied Gunn. "He cut the thong when the fracas started. I was down low, didn't see which direction he took."

"Find Jack Blood!" The old man bellowed, a cold fury in his voice. The contest had been interrupted, the spirits had not been allowed to decide the fate of the two men. The chief turned to Gunn, looked him square in the eyes. "You did not run from your fate. You will stay here, in the tipi of Spotted Horse. When Blood returns, you will fight again . . . fight to the death." The old man threw back his shoulders, returned to his warriors and began barking orders to them.

Red Arrow strode to Gunn's side, untied the hide rope that had begun to chafe the tall man's wrist. "You come, go tipi. The braves will bring Blood soon. But now, you take rest, take food." The young man fell silent as he escorted Gunn to the lodge of the dead brave, Spotted Horse.

Gunn stretched out on the buffalo robe, the same robe that held Fanny a few hours ago. His heart slowed, his breathing returned to normal. He was not hurt badly, a cut or two, superficial. If not for Fanny, he would be dead now. He owed her his life. He smiled grimly. It was ironic. He had come to rescue her, and now she had saved his life. He wondered at such a woman. Stronger than she looked, the blood of a great people ran in her veins. Although he had made a promise to a dying man, was it his place to tamper with life? Perhaps Fanny was with her people, her only relations. Maybe that was the way it should

127

be. Yet her life was no safer than his with the outlaw, Blood, a part of this tribe. Blood. He was the thorn in his side, the cause of all this trouble. The man was pure bad, no good to either red man or white. Blood was gone, and to Gunn, that was an admission of guilt in the murder of Green Willow Leaf. Yet Old Bear did not take it that way. He still wanted the two men to fight to the death. Maybe Blood would not be caught. What then? It was plain that the Cheyenne chief wanted an eye for an eye. If Blood did not return, then would the Indians put him to death and ride on, the deaths of the two braves avenged?

He did not have any answers. He had only weariness and jumbled thoughts like masses of thunderclouds that showed no sign of clearing.

But he hoped the Cheyenne brought Blood back. Alive. Gunn wanted his own fate decided—once and for all.

He closed his eyes, drifted into a light sleep.

It seemed only moments since he had closed his eyes. Red Arrow stood in the gloom of the tipi again. He held something in his hands, a bowl, and the aroma of cooked meat assailed his nostrils.

"Gunn, I bring food and news."

"Yeah, what is it?" Gunn sat up, fully awake now.

"Black Elk stood at place above camp when you fight Blood. He saw you go down, thought you were dead. A little time passed, then he saw Jack Blood pass below him, riding hard toward the north."

"Did the Cheyenne go after him?"

"Yes, but there is more." The young brave lowered

his head, hesitant to relay the news that he'd brought.

"What?"

"There was someone with Blood. A girl. The granddaughter of the chief."

"Fanny? But how? I spoke to Fanny just after the shooting." Gunn was stunned, shocked at the news.

"Blood must have grabbed her, taken her on his horse just after you spoke with her."

Gunn jumped up, crossed the lodge in two steps. "I'm going after her. He'll kill her."

The young man blocked the way. "The chief will not let you go. You must wait for the Cheyenne men to return. They will bring Blood back."

Gunn paused. "You're right, Red Arrow. I don't know, but I feel helpless. That man murdered Green Willow Leaf. He'll murder Fanny, too. He'll use her, then kill her. I've seen his kind before."

"Be patient, my friend. I will bring you what news I can. The women have prepared food. Eat what they bring you. It will nourish you for the fight with Blood. Now, rest well. I will return when I can." The brave did not wait for Gunn to respond. Handing him the bowl of food, he turned and left the man alone.

The minutes passed like hours as Gunn waited. He ate the cooked meat; it tasted like elk, sweet and lean. He knew he must be patient. He still had his knife, sheathed in his boot. He could try and fight his way toward freedom. But breaking out, killing Indians, wouldn't help his cause. Getting himself killed wouldn't help Fanny either.

The afternoon was wearing on when Gunn heard a stirring in the camp. He waited as long as he could for word from Red Arrow, then he decided to see what was going on for himself. Two young guards stood outside the tipi. Gunn made no sudden moves toward them. He stepped outside the lodge as though it were a natural thing for him to do. The two glanced at him, then watched the gathering at the chief's lodge. Riders had come in. Gunn stretched himself up to his full height, but could see no sign of Fanny or of Jack Blood.

Red Arrow broke through the throng, loped toward Gunn, his coarse hair flapping as he ran. The man carried a rifle in his hand, a water bottle slung around his shoulder.

"Gunn, the trackers have lost the sign. Blood has much cunning. He knows the way of the Cheyenne. He has the blood of our tribe. Where many men cannot find him maybe one or two can. I have asked the chief and he has said yes. I will find Jack Blood. And you . . . you will find him. The chief says to go . . . the two of us. We will find Jack Blood and the girl." The young brave was grinning now, grinning with pride at the task he had been awarded.

"The chief trusts me? He is not afraid I will run?"

"He knows you could run now. He say you better man, maybe, than Blood."

Gunn grinned.

"I am grateful to you, Red Arrow. I'll need my horse, rifle and food for two days. We'll find them." Gunn slapped a hand on the man's shoulder.

Red Arrow grinned back.

Fanny bounced along on the blanketed Indian pony, her hands twined into the coarse mane. The

130

man riding behind her had barely spoken. They rode rock ridges, backtracked to cover their trail and stopped once to brush out tracks.

She glanced around, determined to find a means of escape. She could at least try. Blood would probably kill her before the ordeal was over. She could at least have a chance to survive, to get back to Gunn.

The ledge the paint traveled led to a steep, rocky climb. Blood drew the horse to a halt and studied the slope ahead. "We'll stop here for a moment, rest the horse. Don't try anything."

Blood read her mind. Maybe this was her chance to escape. She felt the half-breed's body pull away from behind her. The grip of his arm around her waist relaxed. He dropped to the ground, his heels striking hard.

"All right, girl. Slide down easy."

Fanny wrenched herself free, slipped off the wrong side of the horse. She hit the ground on the opposite side from Blood, her feet in motion almost before they touched down.

"You little bitch!" The half-breed rounded the horse, but not in time to grab the agile girl. She dodged around a boulder, dashed into the undergrowth, disappeared in the thick tangle of bushes. Blood was in pursuit. She could hear him thrashing through the tangled growth. He yelled at her, but she couldn't make out his words.

Fear gripped her, pushed all else from her mind. She had to escape, survive, get back to Gunn.

She scrambled on, stumbling, rising, gasping for breath. Her feet and legs were numb, her hands scratched from brambles. She was growing weak from the ride, the flight, the panic. A pine bough reached out, smacked her across the chest. She reeled, dropped to her knees. Determination drove her back to her feet, sent her plunging onward in the near darkness.

Jack Blood was closing in. His heavy boots crunched the branches, his body swished through the thickets. The sound of his coming was loud. Often he cursed. Sometimes at Fanny, sometimes at the obstacles to the chase. His words echoed across the ravine, bounced off sheer cliff walls.

The words spurred Fanny like a whip, urging her on. Again she tripped, fell. And again she staggered to her feet, driven by sheer terror.

Fanny felt Blood closing in on her, only a step behind her. She could almost feel his huge hands grabbing, clawing her. She bit her lower lip, muffling the urge to scream. Then the scream exploded from her mouth as the murderer's hand brushed against her arm, grabbing, missing. His clumsy lunge was enough for one hand to stretch far enough; it caught the fabric of her sleeve, ripped it. She broke free, ran on for several yards. The terror was a full-blown thing inside her now. The man was like an animal, and in the darkness, she could smell his lust. It was a tangible thing, like a poison on the air, in her heart. Her lungs burned with the fire of burnt oxygen, thin air, and the night closed in on her like a smothering cloak.

"Gunn!" She screamed for the man who was too far away to hear her. Her voice echoed across the rocky bluffs.

Blood propelled himself toward the girl again, this

time catching her, halting her flight. He jerked her around, slammed her to the ground.

"You sneaky little bitch!" he roared. His tall frame hung over her, his chest heaving from the chase. "I'm going to make you sorry you ever heard of Jack Blood! When I get through with you, you can scream for Gunn all you want to. He nor any other man won't want the likes of you."

He reached down, grabbed her arm and jerked her upright. She was limp from exertion, exhausted. There was no fight left in her. She just hung there, suspended by her arm, gasping for breath.

Her mind had exhausted its resources for a plan of escape. She had no strength left in her to run. Blood loomed beside her, so close she could smell his foul breath on her neck. There was no gentleness in his grasp. His fingers dug into the flesh of her arm, shot pain through her limb. She was too breathless now to scream, except in the silence of her mind. Only her thoughts could take her away from this place, out of danger, out of pain.

Her thoughts turned to Gunn. There was sanity there, in these thoughts. Safety. An inner strength began to build in her. She retreated to a center of her being where Blood could not harm her. Gunn would not let her suffer like this. He would come . . . he would save her.

Chapter Fourteen

Gunn found the point where the Cheyenne trackers had lost the trail. He saw how they could lose the spoor in the rocky terrain, but while Red Arrow was following a false trail, the tall man crisscrossed a point where an Indian pony might pick its way over rough ground. Unshod hoof prints lay scattered about in the dust of the rocky landscape, then gathered again for the return to the camp. Somewhere, he knew, Blood would have to leave tracks, and not far off unless he missed his guess. Playing a hunch, he swung wide of the place where the Cheyenne braves had turned back. Then, he began to make a wide circle, hoping to cut a fresh trail in the maze of rocks.

Gunn wiped sweat from his face with his forearm, took off his hat and ran a finger around the sweatband. He replaced the battered felt hat and peered about him, looking for sign. He urged the big sorrel toward what appeared to be an impassable ledge. There he saw what he had been looking for. A moss covered rock, turned at a slight angle. Struck by a passing hoof. Dislodged. The man waved an arm to the mounted rider below.

Red Arrow gained the Walker's side and nodded in agreement at the stone's mark. The Indian swung his mount onto the narrow ledge and led the way up the mountain. Shadows crept out to greet the trackers, limiting their view. The slope grew steeper, rougher. Shadows were beginning to deepen in the eastern pockets, grew long at the higher elevations. There were more stones disturbed, and once Red Arrow pointed to a fresh hoofprint in the dust. The depression had not yet filled in completely, but the edges were starting to blur.

Gunn didn't think of Fanny or of what Blood might be doing to her. He concentrated on keeping to the trail, on finding her. He and Red Arrow were moving much faster than two riders on a single pony. They would have to be sure that they overtook the man and his hostage before harm could be done.

Blood had as much as a four hour start. Four hours. It would be hard to outride such a lead. The country was too rough to gain much time. Still, if they could determine the general direction, stay to the trail even after dark, they had a chance. The darkness was the enemy now. The sun was being swallowed up so that the lowlands were bathed in the gray wash of dusk while the treetops above their elevation glistened golden in the falling sun. Blood, too, was trying to ride with as much daylight as possible, heading west and north. But darkness would come suddenly once the sun fell below the horizon, even in the high country.

Gunn leaned over the big horse, coaxed it with his

rowel-less spurs, trying to gain more speed. The sorrel continued to plod heavily up the steep grade. Esquire was giving it his best, no point in punishing the animal. Maybe Fanny could stall the killer, gain time for herself, for Gunn. She was smart as a whip, he knew, but was she any match for Blood's animal cunning? Only time would tell. Blood was desperate, or he would not have kidnapped the woman he had brought to her grandfather. A desperate man would be capable of doing almost anything to save his own hide. For Blood, this was a last stand. There was no going back now that the truth about Green Willow Leaf had come out.

The two trackers had gained the top of the grade when Gunn heard a noise off to his right. Dry brush rattled. Crackled again. Instinctively, he reined up on the sorrel and dropped quietly to the ground. Red Arrow topped the rise, his head down, eyes scanning the earth for sign.

Gunn crouched, his hand resting on the butt of his pistol. He listened. The crunching rattle came again. The sound of branches brushing against something, someone.

Slipping the weapon from its soft leather sheath, Gunn moved on cat feet toward the noise. The sound came from somewhere behind a jumble of large rocks forming a mound. The dusky air was cool, yet sweat beaded up, slickened the skin on the man's face. He reached the pile of stones, paused and wiped the sweat from his brow.

The mound stood on rock fragments, talus piled up over the years. He couldn't climb it. The footing was too uncertain and the noise he made would be too risky. Gripping his revolver, the tall man eased his way around the rock, his senses alert to his surroundings. This was rough country, perfect for ambush.

Just beyond the pile of rocks, the ground dropped away into a grass-covered gully, deep, treacherous for a lone man on foot. Alert, Gunn scanned the hollow. Darkness cloaked the depression, but close scrutiny revealed the bulky outline of a horse. The animal grazed contentedly in the night air, his rope rein dragging against the brush.

Gunn prowled about the gully, trying to assess why the horse was there, untended. The horse was Cheyenne by the dressing on the throatlatch. It was full dark now, below the rim. Gunn struck a match, crouched to read the footprints. The heavy heel of a man's boot had sunk deep in the summer grass. Those of a lighter person, a girl, perhaps, led off into the brush past the hollow. The match burned out, scorching Gunn's fingers. He was sure now, of what had happened. Fanny had run, maybe escaped. Blood had chased after her. And, he was the stronger, the fleeter of foot. Gunn smiled at her bravery. At least she'd slow Blood down, fight him at every step.

He turned and looked up the slope. The rock cliff shot up, impossible to climb. There was no short cut. He'd have to follow behind, track the pair, try and sneak up on Jack Blood.

The moon rose, shone through the pines now, bounced its light off the sheer bluff. Red Arrow backtracked to the big sorrel, spotted Gunn, waited in the deep shadows.

"Him here," said the Cheyenne.

"Yes," said Gunn. "The girl too. She's running. He

138

means to catch her up."

"We find," said Red Arrow.

"It'll be hard going. On foot."

The Indian dismounted, hefted his rifle. In the darkness, he was a shadow, his dark sleek hair silvered by the moonlight.

Gunn left his rifle in its scabbard, checked his knife. If he did encounter Blood, it would be close work.

They left their horses in the gully, began to move at a trot through the grassy hollow, up the brush-covered slope.

Fanny's feet dragged, the girl so fatigued she scarcely was able to put one foot in front of the other. Jack Blood was one step behind her, urging and prodding her through the tangle of brush. He allowed her no further chance of escape into the darkness. Using her torn dress for a lead rope, the half-breed had ripped the back of the bodice further, twisting the cloth into a leash. The fabric was still attached to the waistline of the girl's dress. The night air chilled the exposed part of her back. Crimson streaks scarred her bare arms where the brush had scratched her.

The bench along which the killer and his hostage traveled began to climb into a grade. The girl staggered, exhausted from the efforts of escape, the sheer physical exertion. Even Blood was beginning to breathe hard. His own strength had been sapped by the running, the chase after the girl. The two knife wounds were not deep, but their raw ache nagged him. Hatred fueled him now, gave him a second wind.

Hatred for Gunn, for the girl who was his unwilling prisoner.

Suddenly, Blood jerked Fanny to a halt, listening. Somewhere ahead, an owl made an eerie sound. Fanny started to move.

"Hold up," the half-breed whispered, his voice harsh in the still air. His hand reached to his waist, to his only weapon, the knife protruding from his belt. He held the leather-bound handle, did not draw the blade. There were no other sounds. The owl hooted again. "Go on," he growled, "it's only a damned hoot owl."

But his voice did not sound sure. It quavered as if he had begun to wonder why an owl was hunting this high in the mountains.

The girl barely heard the first hoot of the owl, but listened intently to the second with alertness, interest. A deep, throaty cry, like a hoarse rooster, she had heard it before at the Cheyenne camp.

The man urged the girl ahead. They pushed on, the girl thrashing the brush as much as she dared, wending her way toward the place where the owl had called. The cry came again, this time ignored by the half-breed, but leading the girl onward, hopeful.

The solitary rifle shot rolled across the night toward Gunn and the Indian brave. They halted at the top of the grade trying to pinpoint the direction of the report. It had come from a considerable distance, somewhere ahead of them in the big pines above the ridge.

"They're still up ahead," Gunn croaked in a half-whisper. "You know if Blood had a rifle when he lit out?"

"The guard who saw him did not speak of a rifle. There would have been word if Blood had many weapons," Red Arrow replied, answering in a hushed voice.

"Then someone else is up there on the mountain." Gunn spoke as much to himself as to his companion.

The two moved forward, stepping lightly toward the direction of the gunshot. They hurried as quickly and as quietly as possible, hoping to gain time or advantage on whatever or whoever lay ahead.

Gunn drew up quickly, held his hand out to halt the brave. "Smoke," the white man whispered. "Smell it?"

Red Arrow nodded his agreement and pointed his rifle in the most likely direction.

Gunn nodded, accepting the man's decision. "Keep moving, easy, until we find out where it's coming from."

The pungent smell of burning wood grew stronger, leading the two trackers on. The pines were thick now, close together. The two dropped behind a fallen tree, waited, watched.

"I can't see a glow, but it has to be down that draw." Gunn held his voice low.

They pushed on quietly, winding in and out of the brush, pausing to crouch behind trees. The tang of the wood smoke grew stronger in their nostrils.

The two edged up to a small rock outcropping. Red Arrow grunted and pointed with his rifle barrel. Gunn could see the glow of a campfire in a small clearing ahead of them. Two figures sat in the light of

141

the flame. But something was wrong. One was a woman. No, they were both women. They sat straight, still.

Gunn motioned for Red Arrow to flank the clearing, come up on the other side. The white man crept forward, alert, cautious.

Closer now, Gunn could see the faces of Fanny and Dancing Star. That one always seemed to turn up at the most unlikely places and at the darndest times.

The two women sat stock still, unmoving.

Gunn could see them clearly now. They were bound. Rags held their hands in their laps and looped downward around their feet.

This was some kind of trap. Jack Blood was out there watching, waiting in the dark.

Gunn eased around the clearing. The shadows behind Dancing Star might conceal him enough to let the women know he was around. The man dropped to his stomach, dragged himself on his elbows toward the stiffened back of the Cheyenne woman. He kept his pistol high, loose in his hand, pulled himself along with his arms. Gunn paused frequently to listen, his own breathing loud in his ears.

He gained ground again and was within a few yards of the shadowed back of Dancing Star.

"Sssst." Gunn exhaled loudly, letting the air whistle over his teeth. "Keep still. Don't turn your head," he whispered.

The Indian woman stiffened slightly.

"Where's Blood?"

"Out there." Dancing Star's words were barely audible. Her head nodded toward Fanny, opposite the fire. Red Arrow's direction.

142

"Listen to me," the man continued. "Don't stare at the fire. It'll blind you when the time comes to run."

The girl nodded, diverted her gaze to the darkened trees straight ahead.

"If I slip you my knife, can you manage to free yourself and then Fanny?"

The upright head bowed forward again.

"The two of you light out of here as fast as you can go. Head back down the trail. Our horses are ground tied in a gully about a half mile back. Blood's horse is with them. Take the pony and go to your father. Red Arrow is here with me. We'll take care of Blood."

Gunn reached for his blade as the cold metal of a gun barrel pressed against his temple.

"Now ain't this cozy?" Jack Blood's voice pierced the quiet night. The rifle pressed deeper into Gunn's flesh. "You folks are mighty accommodating. First, Dancing Star here, brings me a rifle. Of course, she wasn't almighty willing to share it until I convinced her. She got off one shot, but I talked her right out of it. Now you come along so's I don't have to go out hunting for you. Yessir, you folks are mighty accommodating."

Gunn eased his head back slightly to relieve the pressure of the gun on his temple. He cursed himself for the fool. It was plain that Jack was more Indian than white man. He hadn't heard a damned thing. And now, three lives, maybe four, were in jeopardy. Where in hell was Red Arrow? he asked himself.

"Well, now don't you start looking for your Cheyenne friend. He's lying in the bushes over yonder with his head bashed in." Blood chuckled, knowing he had the upper hand.

143

In the moment it took to reverse his grip on the weapon, Blood rammed the rifle butt across Gunn's temple.

A whorl of black clouded the steel-gray eyes, swept Gunn down, down into the empty depths of unconsciousness.

Chapter Fifteen

The gray light of dawn pierced through Gunn's eyelids. Sharp, sickening pains coursed through his head. He remained motionless, eyes closed. Splintered thoughts raced around inside his brain, came rushing at him from all directions.

"Blood," he moaned, struggled to gain an upright position.

Nausea spun queasy wreaths in his gut, whirled in gagging circles. He hung there, his head down, fighting down the bile that threatened to rise up in his throat. He took deep breaths, waited for the dizziness to pass. He opened his eyes to the bleak light.

"Gunn?"

Fanny's voice broke through the sickening cloud. He blinked his eyes, sought her out in the dim haze of morning.

"Gunn, are you hurt bad?" The girl's voice seemed far away, hollow.

He tried to place his hand on his head, touch the source of the pain. But his arms were pinned, heavy.

Gunn shifted his eyes, his gaze traversed the length of his arm. He looked at his hands. They were bound with rags, pieces of the cloth from Fanny's dress.

"You were unconscious for so long," she said. "I was getting worried."

"Blood. Where is he?" Gunn tried to focus his eyes on the girl. She sat erect, her hands and feet still bound. Sometime during the night, Fanny had slipped off her log seat onto the ground. She lay on her side, trussed up like a hanging hunk of cheese. Gunn cursed silently, winced as a fresh pain shot through his head. A wave of nausea flowed through him again.

"I nodded off sometime after he dragged you here and tied you up. When I woke up Blood and Dancing Star were both gone. She must have gotten free, run away. I watched her pick at the bindings, unraveling them. I was so tired and my ties were twisted so tight." Tears began to make silver trails down the dusty cheeks of the bedraggled girl.

"Pull yourself together, girl. Now, think. Have you heard any gunfire?"

The girl shook her head, snuffled.

"Good. That means he probably hasn't caught up with her yet. She might have made it back to the horses, gone for help."

Fanny brightened at the prospect. She watched as the muscular man began to writhe and squirm. He threw his feet upon a downed log and using the stub of a broken branch, began to saw at the cloth that bound his ankles.

Sweat trickled down Gunn's grimy forehead, spattered into his aching eyes. He rested a moment, then continued the relentless, patient rubbing of fabric against wood. The cloth soon frayed enough to weaken it. The strain showed on Gunn's face as he struggled to render the binding into useless strings. With a final jerk, Gunn freed his legs. Now, he kneeled, sawed at his bound wrists. Fanny watched him with wide, pleading eyes. The muscles corded on his neck. The friction sent a thin curl of blue smoke rising from the charred cloth. In a few moments, the threads fell apart. With a mighty tug, he pulled his wrists apart. He unwrapped the strip that connected his hands and feet, rushed to untie the girl.

"Did Blood have an extra rifle?" he asked, working at the knots that held Fanny.

"I didn't see another one. Just the gun Dancing Star had when she tried to shoot him. He took your knife and your pistol. I saw him do that."

Gunn completed the task, leaving the girl to rub at her chafed wrists while he searched the brush for his gun.

Kicking at the fallen leaves and pine straw, Gunn spotted the blue barrel of the Colt near the place where Blood had found him. The half-breed had been careless in his haste to go after Dancing Star.

Grabbing the weapon, Gunn motioned to the girl. "We've got to find Red Arrow, see if he needs help."

The two scoured the brush on the opposite side of the clearing. A sharp gasp from the girl told Gunn what he had feared. Red Arrow lay sprawled in the underbrush, a pool of blood dark under his head

147

and shoulders. The side of the young brave's head was caved in, his brains exposed to the daylight. Black flies had started to swarm, crawling over the terrible wound.

Fanny turned from the sight and retched, the heaves coming from deep inside her. Gunn felt his own nausea begin to resurface.

"Come on," he said, grasping the girl's arm. "We can't do anything for him now. We've got to find Dancing Star. The Cheyenne will take care of him later, give him a proper burial."

"Gunn, I'm so tired I don't know if I can go any farther."

"It means your life, Fanny."

"Yes. Blood . . . he . . . he's mean and cruel."

"Did he hurt you?"

"He didn't have the chance. If Dancing Star hadn't come when she did—" Fanny shuddered.

"Let's go," Gunn said tightly.

The two started down the slope, their legs rubbery from fatigue. It was more difficult, more treacherous going down than it had been climbing up. Often the trail was steep, slippery with loose rock. Sometimes they sat on the slides and let the shifting talus carry them down short stretches of slope. They covered the distance to the gully slowly, Gunn staggering occasionally when the dizziness churned inside his aching head. The sky was clear now, the sun half-way to midday. The way was hot, dusty.

Gunn was relieved to finally see the mound of talus that led to the gully.

"Not far now," he said.

Fanny was too exhausted to reply.

The pair rounded the rock to find the gully washed in sunlight, empty.

The girl dropped to the grass, began sobbing. "I don't think I can go on, Gunn. I'm so tired, so stiff." She rested her head on her arms and wept convulsively. Gunn joined the girl on the grass. He began to stroke her hair, brushed it back from her face. He knew she could not go on like this. The disappointment weighed her down. Each person had his own limits. Fanny had been stretched beyond hers.

"We'll rest awhile. They're on horseback, so we can't catch up. A few minutes' rest won't make much difference." Gunn lay back in the grass, pulled his hat over his eyes and dozed. The rest would do them both good, he reasoned, but he did not drop his guard. His ears strained to pick up any alien sound, any sign of danger. After a moment, Fanny stretched out beside him. Soon, he heard her deep breathing, knew she was sound asleep.

The moon rose clear, bright. Dancing Star watched Gunn's sprawled body, his breathing shallow, his temple bluing from the vicious blow. She wondered if he would live. He looked so pale, his face washed dull and ghostly by the moon's light.

Her mind reeled with anxiety, plans for escape. She feigned sleep, slipping from her upright position into a curled bundle in the dirt. She managed the tumble, putting her back toward Jack Blood.

The half-breed rested against a pine, the girl's rifle across his lap.

Dancing Star shielded her bound hands from

Blood's view and continued to deftly pick at the threads of the fabric binding. She worked for an hour, maybe more, until the cord had frayed into ragged strips of thread. Straining against the remnants, Dancing Star broke the binding, slicing her flesh with the force of her hands pulling apart. She remained coiled, rubbed her bleeding wrists, then smoothly drew her feet within reach of her pained hands. Gingerly, she untied the knots, loosened the cloth from her ankles. She lay there, waiting for her chance.

Jack Blood couldn't stay awake all night.

The half-breed nodded, his head lolling back into the bark of the pine. The touch of the wood aroused him. The camp was unchanged. Gunn was still out cold, his breathing light. Fanny had slipped to a sitting position on the ground, her head drooped close to her chest. Dancing Star was asleep, curled on the ground. Jack tipped his head back, rested it against the tree. Just for a moment.

Dancing Star heard the even breathing coming from behind her. She counted the breaths, synchronized her own with the steady noise. She was sure now that the half-breed was sound asleep.

She would have to leave Fanny. The risk of awakening Blood was too great. And Gunn looked beyond help.

The girl eased herself up on one elbow, not daring to glance at Blood. She continued her fluid motions until she was on her feet. She stole to the side of the clearing, her moccasined feet soundless on the earth and eased into the brush. Careful to make no sound, the girl moved through the growth like a curl of

150

smoke. She stopped frequently to listen for sounds of pursuit. None came.

Sure she was out of earshot, Dancing Star began to edge in the direction of the gully that Gunn had described. A careless moccasin crunched down on a dry twig. The girl's heart stopped. Then it came, thrashing in the brush. Jack Blood had heard her, was awake; he was after her.

Dancing Star raced down the slope, toward the hiding place Gunn had described. The moonlight guided her. The grade, the rocky slope. The girl half-ran, half-slid down the incline. A horse nickered, stamped a hoof on moist soil. Ahead she saw a swell of rock and brush outlined in the moonlight.

Without breaking her pace, the Indian girl circled the mound, grabbed the rope rein and swung herself onto the back of the paint. The other two horses reared their heads, their ears flicking, twitching. The pony hesitated, then responded to the girl as she clapped her heels hard into its flanks. The rider swung the horse onto the trail, headed down the mountain.

Jack Blood cursed himself for his carelessness. He had no plan, no men to help. The girl could not be allowed to reach Old Bear's camp. The whole tribe would come after him, would find him now.

"Damned Injun bitch," he muttered. "Should have killed her when I first saw her sneak up on me."

But it was too late for hindsight. The Indian was gone, and she knew these mountains better than he did. Still, he could overtake her, shut her mouth permanently. That was the only way. He could take care of Gunn and Fanny later.

151

The plan blossomed in his mind.

He reached the gully and mounted Gunn's big sorrel, grabbing the reins of the spare horse. At least Gunn and the girl would not be able to follow him, even if the man was in any condition to ride.

He listened to the pounding hooves of the unshod Indian pony, knew where Dancing Star was. He rammed spurs into the Walker's flanks, felt the horse's muscles bunch as it leaped under the saddle.

The fleeing girl guided the horse gingerly down the slope, the animal leaning back on its haunches to keep its balance. The girl tried to prod the animal, but the footing was precarious. The horse kept its own head, its own pace. Rocks clattered occasionally from far up the trail. Blood was close, too close. The girl would have to run the horse flat out, once level ground was reached.

The trail became easier, broke through the pines and rolled into a meadow. The girl gripped the horse with her knees and lay flat along his shoulder. The pony broke into a gallop, its coarse mane whipping the girl's face.

The pale moonlight made the shadows bristle through the pines as she streaked through them, trusting the horse now, letting the animal dodge the obstacles in its path. The girl urged the animal on, faster. Her heart raced in time to the hoofbeats. She didn't look back, didn't want to know how close the killer rode.

Wild anger and hate filled the half-breed. The girl was ahead, riding hard. He glimpsed the flank of the paint through the trees. The moon's light washed the trail, floured it with a bone-white dust. The way ahead was clear of pines, clear of thickets.

The man could see her now, a few dozen yards ahead. His horse kept pace with the fleeing Indian pony, gained a little. The half-breed balanced the rifle in his hand, raised it to his shoulder. He synchronized his movements with that of his horse, getting his timing, his pace. The killer slouched forward slightly, brought his free hand up for support and sighted down the long blue barrel. He squeezed the trigger, felt the punch of the butt into his shoulder.

The rifle spit flame, threw its thunder at the fleeing girl. The sound rolled over her, chilled her blood.

Suddenly the paint fell away from under her. The ground slammed into her body. The horse screamed in pain, thrashed its legs, struggled to rise.

It floundered there, bleeding from a wound in its side. Dancing Star tumbled clear of the wounded animal, gained her feet and broke into a choppy run. She worked her way toward a shadowy formation that lay ahead. A rock outcropping.

She reached the site, dropped to her knees and crawled in close to the rock. She lay immobile, the ground warm against her body. Her breath came fast, her muscles ached from the fall. The sound of her own heart drowned out all else. Time passed slowly. The darkness was her haven, her immobility made her invisible. The rock protected her, hid her from sight.

She cowered there until her heart stopped beating like the wings of a caged bird, until her breath leveled off and the fire in her lungs subsided.

It was quiet.

She was safe.

Finally she stirred, slid backwards from under the rock.

She breathed the clean air of freedom.

In the next instant she felt a hand clamp firmly over her mouth.

Chapter Sixteen

Dancing Star stiffened with fright. She struggled to tear the vise-like fingers from her lips. She wiggled, twisted in her blind panic. She grabbed the muscular wrist that held her, struck out wildly with her free hand. The hard body weighed heavy against her, crushed the breath out of her lungs. She tried to bring her knees up, push him away. He pressed tighter against her. Her elbows dug into his chest. Suddenly she became aware of a voice, a low whisper in her ear.

"Dancing Star, it's me. It's Gunn. Don't cry out."

Exhausted, her chest heaving with every breath, the Indian girl shuddered as the fear drained away from her. Her knees shook as she drew back to focus on the face that only inches from her own. The morning light crept over the horizon, brightened her refuge and lit the features of the tall white man.

"You all right?" asked Gunn.

She nodded.

"Where's Blood?" he asked.

The girl shrugged. "He's there. Somewhere out there." Her breath quavered from the after-effects of

155

her fright, but she continued. "Blood shot the pony. I fell, unhurt and found this place. It was dark. How long?"

"You've been here about two hours, I reckon. Have you heard anything?"

"Nothing," replied the girl. "But he is here. The birds do not sing, the crow does not call. He is near, waiting."

"Yeah," he said quietly. "That's my hunch, too."

He didn't tell Dancing Star how close she had come to getting killed. He had heard her breathing before he saw her in the rocks. Every nerve jangled, every instinct told him to shoot first, but that was not Gunn's way. He had learned long ago, in the hills and hollows of the Arkansas Ozarks, to be sure of his target before shooting. But Blood had him running ragged. When he knew it was Dancing Star in the rocks, he thought she might be a decoy, but then, as the dawn light brought her huddled figure into stark relief, he saw that she was hiding. Blood would have had her sit in full view, or staked out like an animal while he waited in ambush.

Gunn edged his way from beneath the rock overhang, kept low to the warming earth. The girl scuttled out beside him, lay flat, followed the man's example. She turned her head toward him and spoke quietly. "Where is my sister's daughter?"

"She's up there." He nodded in the direction of a brushy knoll some fifty yards up the mountainside. "I set her in a thicket, made her swear not to twitch a muscle." Gunn began to move ahead, slowly. The pistol in his hands glittered in the sun.

The pair crept toward the tangled thicket, stopped

occasionally to wait, listen. At the brushy knoll, Gunn kept his voice low. "Fanny," he called, waited for a reply. There was no answer.

He called again. "Fanny." He listened, heard no breathing from within the thick growth. He reached out and parted the brush that covered her hiding place.

She was gone.

Gunn's blood froze. A muscle twitched in his jaw. He strained to hear any alien sound. The log where he had left her sitting was empty. The log was damp with dew, except for a round place where it was dry.

Dancing Star watched the man's face intently, then, out of the corner of her eye she saw something, a mark on the ground. She made a soft grunt from deep within her throat, pointed to the spot.

There beside the log on which Fanny had been left to wait was a heel print, a man's boot mark, deep in the moist soil. The two got to their feet, began to search the area for sign. Another footprint lay at the edge of the thicket. Somebody had crushed through the growth leaving broken twigs in his wake.

Gunn and the girl stooped over the leaves, scouring the earth for more prints.

"Gunn!" A voice bellowed across the mountain, bounced against the rock bluffs, echoed down the hillside. "I have the girl!" Blood's voice rolled at the two from somewhere above them. But the terrain broke the sound up, so that Gunn could not pinpoint Blood's exact location. His palms began to sweat, the pistol butt turned slick in his hand.

Gunn stood and scanned the craggy rock above him. The glare of the rising sun worked against him, made him squint his eyes.

"Up here!" Jack Blood yelled again.

Dancing Star shaded her eyes, scanned the high ridges.

"There they are," said Gunn tightly.

Gunn spotted the breed and the girl above him. Blood gripped Fanny about the waist with one arm, held a knife to her throat with his free hand. The killer and his hostage stood on the rim of a rock ledge several hundred yards up the face of the mountain. The light morning breeze batted the girl's tattered skirt about her legs, blew coarse black hair around her face. The tip ends of her braids flapped loosely over her shoulders. She was too far away for Gunn to see the expression on her face, but her flesh was pale and Gunn could sense her fear even from this distance.

"You and the squaw come on up here, Gunn. We need to parlay. Drop the pistol, keep your hands above your belt. You make one slip and the girl gets her throat slit. Remember Goodsmith?"

The tall man nodded and put the Colt behind a rock. He spoke low to Dancing Star as he passed. "After I start up, you pick up that pistol. I'll block his view. I'll trip and stagger. That'll be the time you bend over, pick it up quick. Bring it with you. Keep far enough back so that he can't keep an eye on both of us at the same time. When I get up there, you come up behind me quick, put the butt of that pistol in my hand. Think you can do it?"

"Yes," Dancing Star hissed, her eyes glittering, a half-smile playing on her lips.

"Now, Gunn!" Blood shouted. "Move!"

Gunn waved a hand in acknowledgment, began to make his ascent of the rocky hillside. Dancing Star paused, allowed Gunn to climb a few yards ahead of her. She saw him stumble, fight to keep his balance. Quickly, she scrambled toward the rock, snatched up the pistol and brought it up inside her buckskin shirt. She grasped the weapon by the barrel, held it tight against her belly. Gunn half-spun, flailed his arms as if walking a tightrope.

"Talk to me, Gunn. Thrash the brush. I want to hear you coming up the hill."

"I'm talking, Blood. What do you have to say to me?"

"Keep a-comin'."

"You can do better than that."

"Mister, I want to see your eyeballs real close. You get your ass up here or this breed squaw gets six inches of blade in her craw." Blood's tone was flat, stony, without an ounce of pity in it.

Gunn took a breath, steeled himself for the rest of the climb. He did not look back at Dancing Star, but heard her panting for breath, heard her moccasins whisper over pebbled earth. He had a chance to take Blood. A slim chance. It was always tough to deal with a crazy man. Blood was as knotty as a scrub pine.

"Just keep a-comin' there," Blood said again.

Gunn struggled to gain a steep rise. His bootheels wobbled on the uncertain footing. He was close enough now to hear the breeze flapping Fanny's dress, but he could not see her. "You okay, Fanny?"

"Sure, she's okay, Gunn. I treat the ladies with respect, don't I, little girly?" The breed nuzzled his

159

chin against the girl's cheek, gripped her tighter about the waist. Fanny struggled against Blood's grasp, her foot slipping on the loose rock. Blood's knife point slit a tiny nick in the girl's smooth throat. A fine trickle of blood etched a path along a wrinkle in her soft flesh.

"Now, look at what you made me do, girly." The man slid his finger along the red trickle and held the smeared tip for Fanny to see. The terror that had held the young girl for so long, overwhelmed her, sucked the blood from her head, turned her face chalk. She slipped into a dead faint.

"Damnit, girly. This is a helluva time for you to be getting weak-kneed on me." Blood half-muttered to himself as he dragged the limp body of the girl away from the rocky ledge. Gunn saw them now, saw Fanny fall into a deep swoon. He cursed inwardly, but then realized that this might be the break he needed. With Fanny unconscious, he would have to deal only with Blood.

Gunn watched the man, knew the girl was unharmed, and continued his trek up the slope. Dancing Star held back, faltered in her climb.

"Dancing Star, can you hear me?" Gunn whispered.

"I hear, Gunn."

"What's that you say, Gunn?" Jack Blood's voice was tinged with suspicion.

"Just checking on the Indian girl behind me, Blood."

"Well, you two just keep coming. Don't try no funny stuff."

Gunn spoke fast and low. "When we get close, you

come up behind me with that pistol. Keep clear of Fanny." Gunn kept his eyes trained on the half-breed above him, hoped Dancing Star heard his words.

Blood carried the limp Fanny to a boulder. The small frame of the girl was draped over the half-breed's arm. Her head lolled downward, loose like a rag doll.

Keeping in Gunn's shadow, Dancing Star switched the pistol to her right hand, pointed the barrel downward. She followed the tall man by five or six paces, never taking her eyes off the half-breed.

Thirty paces away, Gunn made his move. He started toward Blood, crouched as if to tackle the man. Blood backed away from the menacing rush. It was an instinctive move, one that Gunn counted on. Then he stopped, backed up toward Dancing Star.

"Now!" yelled Gunn, diving into the brush just off the rocky trail.

Dancing Star, without thinking, squeezed off a shot. The barrel spewed orange flames. The acrid stench of gunsmoke boiled over the shoulders of the Indian girl, filled her nostrils, her eyes.

"Throw me the pistol," he rasped, his gaze fixed on the Indian maid. He saw that she was transfixed, blinded by the blowback of hot powder, the white cloud of smoke.

Dancing Star did not reply. She did not move.

"Get down!" Gunn yelled.

Dancing Star stood stock-still, an easy target for the killer on the ridge. The pistol in her hand began to drop. She was a good half dozen yards away from Gunn, exposed, in the open. In his position, he could no longer see Blood.

Jack Blood heard the bark of the gun, the whine of the bullet. A hot shaft of pain pierced his shoulder, burrowed into his knife wound. His reflexes twanged like a broken guitar string and he dropped the limp girl onto the ground. Her tattered form crumpled to the rocky shelf. Blood crouched low, reached for his rifle that lay beside him on the ground. He shouldered the weapon, wincing as the butt sent pain shooting down his wounded arm.

He took aim, squeezed off a shot. The rifle spit lead toward the still-frozen Indian girl. She saw the flash from the rifle barrel, its deadly orange blossom. She felt the hot sear of leaden fire in her side. Dancing Star smiled at the thought of the desert flowers she would see again in summer, then she sank to the rocky trail. Blackness swirled around her, swallowed her up. Gunn's pistol clattered on the rocks.

Jack Blood saw the girl go down, saw the pistol skid through the gravel. Before he could react, he saw a man's arm shoot out from the brush, grasp the pistol butt. The pistol and the arm disappeared. He heard the Colt's hammer cock, an ominous scrape of metal in the stillness following the explosion of his own rifle.

"You double-crossing bastard," he cursed. The brush below rattled like wind through reeds and then it was quiet. Blood swallowed a hard lump in his throat.

The breed held his crouch and cast his eyes about for cover, for escape. One girl was in a faint, one dead or near-dead and only Gunn and the weapon was out there. And his shoulder hurt, was bleeding freely.

Blood searched, spotted a slide just off the ridge. The talus was a rough way out, but it might gain him the time he needed.

The half-breed kept low and backed toward the loose rock. He eased himself over the edge and tucking into a sitting crouch, began to slide down the sharp, loose rock to safety.

Gunn heard rock scattering and eased out of the brush. Dancing Star lay sprawled across the trail. The man felt her throat for a pulse. Life flickered lightly, unevenly in the woman's frail body. Gunn gently moved Dancing Star into a more comfortable position and gingerly tore the buckskin dress away from the wound. The bullet had punched a hole just under the rib cage. Running his fingers around her back, he could feel no exit wound. The whole thing looked bad. The bullet was still in her, could be lodged in a vital organ.

Fanny drew herself up to a sitting position atop the rise, conscious now. She looked vacantly at the wounded woman below her. The girl staggered to her feet, shook her head to relieve the fuzzy feeling and stumbled down the rise to Gunn's side.

"You see anything of Blood up there?" he asked.

"Nothing. Looks like he slid down the slope. I came to in time to hear the gunfire, but I dared not move. I kept my eyes closed, heard Blood slide down the loose rock. He could already be in that valley down there," the girl paused. "Is she dead?"

"No, but she's hurt bad. We've got to get her back to the village. She won't live out the day up here. I can pack her wound with leaves, with mosses, but that's just temporary. We've got to build a drag and get her to her people."

Fanny looked at Dancing Star's face. The flesh flickered as though a hidden pain coursed through her. She turned away, brushed at sudden tears that welled up in her eyes.

The two worked swiftly. Gunn uprooted young saplings, trimmed them with his knife. At his instructions, Fanny gathered small pine boughs. Gunn used the girls' braid bindings, strips of her buckskin dress to lash the poles together, weave branches together for the litter. The device was fashioned after the travois. The shaft poles were longer than the trailing ones and the platform was just sturdy enough for the light weight of the wounded girl.

Loading the unconscious Dancing Star onto the makeshift litter, the two used the travois like a stretcher until they could gain level ground. There Gunn centered himself between the long shafts and pulled his delicate load toward the sunset and the camp of Old Bear and his Cheyenne.

Chapter Seventeen

Jack Blood was tired of running and hiding. His muscles throbbed with pain every time he moved. His nerves screamed for rest, tore at his senses like razor-toothed bats on a ravenous, screeching attack. Every sound jangled his nerve-ends until the pain in his head was a living thing, a thunderous club that pounded his brain incessantly. He saw the cotton-woods ahead, a sure sign of water, staggered toward the grove, tripping in tall grasses, stumbling over unseen rocks. He packed his flesh wound with mud from the creek that trickled through the little valley. He let his sore feet soak in the bubbling stream, felt some of the soreness seep out in the ripples that massaged his soles. The wound was not as bad as he had thought. The bullet passed through clean and the bleeding had stopped. Such a wound would heal quickly in the high, mountain air. He lost strength steadily, but his anger grew. Gunn had ruined his plans.

He hated him for that. He would kill a man for much less. Gunn was the goddamned sand in the axle grease, the fly in the buttermilk.

The half-breed wanted to live among the Cheyenne, to be safe from the white man's law and the soldiers. Fanny had been his passage to Old Bear's heart. Then Gunn showed up and put a kink in his rope. Blood hated the white man more than he had ever hated anyone. He wanted revenge.

He wanted to soak his hatred in Gunn's blood, see the man suffer. He wanted to twist a knife through his gut, gouge out his eyes. He knew ways to kill a man, ways that would take a long time, make a man scream and weep and beg for death. He thought about those ways now, as he lay by the stream bank regaining his strength.

With only a sharp knife, Blood could torture a strong man like Gunn for hours, reduce him to the level of a whimpering animal. He could ram the knifepoint under each fingernail until the blood ran. He could prick his flesh a thousand times, let him slowly bleed to death. He could cut off his fingers, his scrotum, his toes. He would die, but he would die slowly and with much pain. That was the way to kill a man like Gunn. Make him suffer, make his eyes dull over with pain.

Blood's urgency to escape grew dimmer. Now he wanted to fight, to kill Gunn. But first he needed food and rest. There was a big stand of spruce at the edge of the meadow, thick and dark, offering both shelter and concealment. He limped through the elk-trodden grasses, following their traces in order to leave behind no spoor. The wounded man settled himself into the grove, crawled back into the deepest part, snugged himself between a pair of trunks. He lay back, closed his eyes. The ground was soft here, and the fatigue drained out of him, flowed into the earth. Jack Blood slept deeply, the sleep of a man who had made a decision, a man satisfied with himself. He awoke several hours later, walked on firmer legs to the stream and drank deeply from the little creek, ate berries and roots that grew on the outer edges of the spruce thicket. He rested, gained strength for his meeting with Gunn. As he became stronger, his hatred for Gunn grew deeper.

There was silence across the land. The coming dusk began to pull long tree shadows across the mountain meadows. Aspen stood like sentinels, stark white among the pine, spruce and fir trees, as Gunn pulled the litter along behind him, his muscles working easily, his lungs filling out as he breathed, expanding his chest. Occasionally a rock caused one of the dragging poles to lift, jostling the wounded girl. Moans escaped her parched lips at such times, but she did not regain consciousness. The fever raged within her, sweat beaded up on her forehead. He and Fanny stopped often to make sure Dancing Star was comfortable. The frequent stops slowed them down so that they made little progress. Always, Gunn would scan the surroundings, listening, searching for any movement, any sign of Blood.

The sun slipped behind the mountains, leaving a splash of color along the rim. A stream rustled over rocks ahead of the slow moving caravan when Gunn decided to make camp for the night. The pair had traveled only a mile and a half, maybe two. Fanny looked after Dancing Star, making her comfortable on the makeshift litter, while Gunn gathered saplings, stripped aspens of bark, built a fire and set about making a bark vessel for boiling water. The man had lived on the land and knew its ways much as the Indians did. If he kept the lick of the flame below the level of the water in the bark cup, the bark would not catch fire.

"Do you know the roots the Cheyenne use for medicine?" Gunn asked.

"Yes, some. My mother . . ." She hesitated, choked on a sob in her throat. "My mother taught me many of the old ways."

"There is a plant the Cheyenne use to stain their porcupine quills. I have heard it's also a medicine."

"What do you call it?" she asked.

"Bloodroot, I think. It's a kind of dock that grows here in these mountains."

Fanny's brows wrinkled in thought. Creases latticed her forehead. Gunn trimmed the fire, poured water into the bark bowl. He made a fire ring of stones, began to cut saplings, two forked ones, a single straight stick to place between them.

"Yes," she said finally, "I know this plant. The Cheyenne call it *maheskoe mahetseiyo*. This is the red medicine that steeps, the bloodroot that stops the bleeding."

Gunn searched his memory. He had spent time among the Lakota, and knew some Cheyenne friends from those days. The Indians, he knew, could find all the medicines they needed among the plants and roots that grew on the plains, in the mountains.

"I think that's it," he said. "See if you can find

some bloodroot plants and . . ."

"I know them, where to find them. I have seen my mother boil them, use the liquid to color porcupine quills. But as a medicine, she used to pound the dried root to powder and put a pinch of it in boiling water."

"We can dry the roots on the fire," Gunn said. "Hurry before it gets too dark to see."

Fanny did his bidding, hurrying off to search for the bloodroot plant. She returned with several as the darkness settled into the meadow. Gunn dried the plants on the stones that ringed the fire. He put together his spit, hung roots from it. He took the driest plant, gave it to Fanny. She put the plant in the hollow of a stone, used a round, smaller stone, to mash the root, pulverize it. The water boiled and she added the powder to the pot. She managed to get a few drops of the medicine past Dancing Star's cracked lips. Sure that the wounded girl was resting easy, Fanny set about the camp, working in the ways that her Cheyenne mother had taught her.

"I will feed her this medicine until she has drunk it all," she said.

Gunn stood beyond the firelight, making another bowl from aspen bark. He soaked the bark in water, formed the shape, toasted the dampness out over the fire. The bowls were crude and small, but they held water. He made two more, filled them with water, set them close to the fire. Fanny gathered service berry leaves, put them in the water.

Night erased the forms and shadows of the dusk as Gunn finally settled himself with a bark cup of tea made from the berry leaves Fanny had found. He had tasted such before, knew they were used in ceremonials.

"What do you call this tea?" he asked.

"My mother called this male berry *hetanimins*. They are sacred to the Cheyenne, but sometimes we would drink it. Is it good?"

"Yes. It tastes like green tea."

His mind was drifting over the day's events when he heard the sound.

It was like a rasp, a hoarse cough. Fanny sat up, alert, frightened.

Gunn grinned, held his fingers to his lips to quiet Fanny. Motioned for her to stay and slipped into the pitch of the surrounding night.

Fanny sat stone still. She waited, but did not know what she was waiting for. A gunshot? A fight? Then the thrashing came. The bushes heaved and crackled.

Gunn burst through the growth leading the big sorrel. Tied to the horn of the Walker's saddle was the lead rope for the paint that followed.

The girl giggled with relief. "How did you know?" she questioned.

"Well," Gunn motioned toward a dark knoll. "I knew it couldn't be too far away. These two were listening for us just as much as I was listening for them. I figured we'd catch up to them sooner or later." The man patted the big horse on the neck.

Gunn unsaddled the sorrel, rubbed the animal carefully with a handful of leaves. The animal had worn the saddle for two days with no relief. A man had to take care of his horse. Often a good horse could mean the difference between life and death.

Finishing with Esquire, Gunn took the blanket off the Indian pony and curried its spotted back.

He tethered the two horses within reach of the stream and its lush grass and returned to the camp to share the food from his saddlebags with the hungry young girl.

"We all need plenty of rest, Fanny. Let's stay here tonight. Dancing Star will get a chance to gain some strength. We can set out early. We'll hitch the drag to the Indian pony and make good time. Esquire can carry us double. Maybe we can get to the Cheyenne camp by sundown."

Fanny nodded her agreement. She welcomed the rest. The day had been an exhausting tramp down the mountain. The girl fell into a sound sleep as soon as she rolled up in the blanket Gunn laid out for her.

Dawn turned her gray haze to a blush of pink lighting the way for the small caravan that plodded toward the Powder River encampment. The Indian pony pulled the travois, somehow aware of the delicate burden. The big Walker was rested, anxious to move down the trail. The tall man and the half-breed girl rode together, his arm tucked lightly around her tiny waist.

Jack Blood stirred at the first show of light. His shoulder pained, but his strength was growing. His anger, his need for revenge pushed him forward out of the grove and into the waiting arms of two Cheyenne braves.

A tall youth rolled his shoulder into Blood's side, knocking the breed to the ground. The rifle dropped to the dirt, bounced across a rock out of reach. Blood tried to get up, but was held down by a heavy moccasined foot resting on his belly. The half-breed swore at the two, struggled fruitlessly.

The wounded man was pulled to his feet, managed to free one arm. He swung his good arm savagely at his nearest captor, struck the Cheyenne across the face. Running Deer grabbed his jaw, startled, let out a low moan. Two more braves joined the wounded one. Blood struggled in vain against the increased confinement.

The four Cheyenne surrounded Blood, secured each wrist with long rawhide thongs. Two of the braves mounted their horses and were handed the thongs, one rider on each side of the prisoner. The wounded Indian, Running Deer, strode forward and slipped a noose of rawhide over Blood's head and down around his neck. Running Deer, his eye beginning to discolor, took up the lead thong. The boy nodded to the mounted braves.

The two holding the rawhide that bound Blood's wrists eased their horses in opposite directions, stretching the half-breed's arms out, wrenching the sockets. Pain shot up his damaged shoulder. This was not a torture he had thought about using on Gunn. The pain was excruciating.

The Indian with the lead rope stood close to the breed. Blood swung his leg out, caught Running Deer in the groin. The two mounted Indians laughed at the unfortunate brave. The young man gripped his crotch, peered out of his swelling eye at the prisoner. Hatred contorted the Cheyenne's face.

The hide around Blood's throat drew up tight, cutting into the breed's fleshy neck.

The two riders clucked to their mounts and the

172

four braves headed toward Old Bear's camp with their much-sought-after prize.

Jack Blood stumbled on the loose rock, trying to pace himself with the horses. He could not gain his footing and was dragged a few yards. The fourth Cheyenne kicked the downed man, then grasped his belt and pulled him onto his feet. Blood staggered, then got his timing right. He trotted along beside the two ponies.

The braves laughed among themselves and occasionally jerked on their reins, sending the bound man lurching forward or backward between them. Pain surged through the half-breed's arm. Blood trickled from the open wound. He clung to his anger, his hatred for Gunn. The hate left no room for pain or fear.

Running Deer turned frequently to gaze at the prisoner. Old Bear would be pleased. The spirits would not be cheated of the vengeance owed for Spotted Horse and Red Eagle.

Throughout the morning, Blood trotted, struggled to keep up. His feet, pounded and mashed to pulp, bled through crushed pores. The ground grew rockier. Running Deer contributed to the prisoner's exertion, jerking the lead thong, tripping the staggering man. Hatred kept the half-breed alive, moving. Gunn was ahead of him somewhere, maybe already in the Cheyenne camp, waiting, waiting to die.

Jack Blood awoke. He lay face down on rocky ground, his hands tied behind his back. He could hear the sound of voices, many Indian voices. A dog barked nearby. He tried to raise his eyelids. His red-rimmed eyeballs ached in the midday light. He had had no food, no water. His tongue lay swollen behind his cracked, bleeding lips.

A nudge in his ribs rolled him over. He squinted at the face of Old Bear, above him.

"You lie in the dirt like a coward, Jack Blood. Stand on your feet like a man." The chief kicked the half-breed again, this time with more effort.

The prisoner let out a grunt, tried to roll to his knees, to stand. Blood's eyeballs screamed in pain at the glare of the early sun.

"Where's Gunn?" he asked, balancing himself on his knees.

"You do not ask about Dancing Star. You have wounded my youngest daughter and you have no concern for her?" The old man turned his back on the half-breed, walked away from the small clearing.

"It was self-defense," Blood yelled at the man's back. "She tried to kill me." The words fell away, ignored by the departing chief.

A hard thrust to his back sent Blood sprawling in the dirt. He lifted his head, tried to rise. Running Deer set his foot in the middle of Blood's back and pushed him down, his face grinding into the rocky ground.

"You red sonuvabitch! I'll kill you for this!" Blood shouted, spitting dust at the young brave.

Running Deer laughed. His hand held a water gourd. The brave tipped his wrist letting the precious liquid spatter in the dust. He emptied the water onto the ground, laughed at Blood's attempt to catch a few drops in his mouth.

"You will fight the white man, Gunn. And if you win, then I will fight you, Jack Blood. You will die. Running Deer does not fight like a white man, Jack Blood. And you are not a white man. You are not Indian. I am an Indian and I will fight to kill my enemy, any way I can."

The young Cheyenne spat in Blood's direction, walked away.

Blood glared after him. Then, as he realized what the brave had said, his stomach knotted in fear.

Chapter Eighteen

During the long night, Gunn and Fanny fed Dancing Star the bloodroot broth, saw her fever flare and diminish, flare again. They kept the fire going, made more of the medicinal tea, fed it to the wounded Indian girl a tiny mouthful at a time. Gunn watched as Fanny cooled the broth with her breath, let the fluid seep past Dancing Star's lips. He saw the Cheyenne maid choke, gasp for breath while something tore at his insides.

He remembered that her father, Jacques Laurent lived for years among the Cheyennes, one of the few to be accepted among the tribe. He had taken Green Willow Leaf for a wife, made her heavy with child. Fanny had spent her earliest years with the Northern Cheyennes, then had gone to join the Southern branch along the Smoky Hill. The latest trouble between whites and Indians had brought the two tribes back together, joining the Sioux to keep the settlers out of the last good hunting grounds. Ten years before, her father had fought with the Cheyennes, left with the Southern tribe to hunt the Smoky

Hill in the Spring of '66. Gunn had heard him tell of riding with Gray Beard, Bull Bear, Tall Bull, White Horse, the Bent brothers and the great war leader, Roman Nose. They went to join Black Kettle below the Arkansas. When they reached the valley of the Smoky Hill, they found stragglers who had run away from the camps of Black Kettle and Little Raven, discovered that they had signed a treaty in 1865, giving up tribal rights to their old hunting grounds.

Gunn remembered hearing of those hard days from Fanny's father, but her mother never mentioned them. Later, he learned she had lost a brother at the Washita ford fight, and there were times when he heard her softly weeping at the bad memories of those times. Fanny was a child, then, no more than nine or ten summers, he recalled.

"I was with 'em that day," Jacques had told him. "Camped up on the Arikaree. Green Willow Leaf and little Fanny was with me. 'Bout three hundred braves, Hollow Pine, Leaf's brother among 'em. It was what the Cheyenne call the Moon When the Deer Paw the Earth, September, I think, and some Sioux from Pawnee Killer's camp jumped about fifty white men. Some of Wynkoop's special scouts. They come roarin' back into camp, all excited and yelling, saying we had better get up some war parties and kill these scouts. They was camped on the Arikaree, 'bout twenty mile below us. Some of them wore blue coats, but most was dressed in buckskins.

"Some of Pawnee Killer's runners come into our camp and got everyone all fired up. Tall Bull and White Horse sent out runners to the Cheyenne camps and pretty soon everyone was breaking out the war

178

rigs and painting up for battle. I 'member Leaf's brother, Hollow Pine bein' one of those who went to get Roman Nose. He was in his lodge gettin' purified. His medicine had been hurt by eatin' some Sioux bread that was cooked with an iron fork. He said he would join the war party soon as he finished purifying hisself."

"What was his medicine?" Gunn asked.

"He had magic power so that white men's bullets couldn't touch him. Anyways, all the rest of us rode out, the Cheyenne wearin' their crow bonnets, the Sioux in eagle feathers, quite a sight. The old chiefs warned everybody not to attack in small bunches. They wanted to ride right over them scouts like Roman Nose told 'em to do and wipe ever' one of 'em out. But some of the young bucks got eager, and run in there, tried to run off the scouts' horses. They only got a few and the whites grabbed the rest, holed up on a little island out in the middle of the river. They was in high grass and in amongst the willer trees, so it was pure hell findin' a target. They had repeatin' Spencers, too, and every time a bunch of braves would charge, they'd get slowed up in the river and those Spencers would tear hide and skin bark."

"Did Leaf's brother get killed there?"

"Yeah, he did, in the same charge when Roman Nose got killed. He lost his magic I guess. He got a ball in the spine, lay out in the brush all day, crawled up the bank come nightfall. Some of the braves carried him up to high ground, but he died anyway. Like he knew he would."

Gunn knew of the incident. The whites called it the Battle of Beecher's Island. The Indians kept the scouts holed up on the island for eight days. They were eating their dead horses, digging in the sand for water. The stench of rotting flesh was so strong, the Indians finally went away. Lieutenant Frederick Beecher was killed there, and so the fight was named after him. The Indians did the same thing. They called it The Fight When Roman Nose Was Killed, and it was the darkest day for the Cheyennes.

"In the morning, I will be able to find other roots and herbs that will help cure Dancing Star," said Fanny, breaking into his thoughts.

"You don't think she should be moved? Back to the Cheyenne camp?"

"No."

Gunn looked at the sky, felt the building wind. The moon was rising, its luminous hulk gauzed over with mist, a halo surrounding it. He cursed, stood up, walked away from the ring of firelight. He sniffed the air, tasted its dampness on his tongue.

"It's going to rain," he said. "I'll have to build a shelter."

"No," said Fanny softly. "I know this place. My father and mother brought me here a few years ago. Beyond this meadow, higher up, there is a large cave, made when the rocks fell."

Gunn stalked back to the fire.

"How far?"

"It is no more than an hour's walk, faster on a horse."

Four miles, he thought.

"Could you find it in the dark?"

"Yes. There is an old path, where a boulder rolled through the forest. It is wide and easy. My father told me the Cheyenne used to come there to make medicine, but their enemies found it and it was too easy for them to come up that path and make war on the people. No one has been there in many years. The people consider it now a place of bad medicine."

Gunn had never heard of it, but he knew such places existed. The Cheyenne were a spiritual people and they made much of medicine places. If Dancing Star was to survive, then it was worth a try. A cave would give them shelter and perhaps speed the healing process. He did not yet know how badly the Indian maid was hurt. Maybe she had wounds inside. If so, then moving her too much might kill her. Fanny was probably right. It would be best to hole up for a few days. Meanwhile, however, Blood was out there somewhere, free to do his dirty work.

"I'll saddle my horse, and hook up the travois," he said. "You do what you can to make her comfortable."

Fanny let out a sigh, nodded, her face flickering with bronze light from the campfire.

At that moment, Gunn thought, she looked more Cheyenne than half-breed.

Something big had cut a swath through the trees all right. A meteor, maybe, or a landslide. The trees had not grown back because there was rock strewn thick and deep along the path. It was slow going, and the travois bounced too much, but it was not far to the cave. Gunn saw Fanny pull up before he saw the sheer mass of mountain wall before him. Even in the dim moonlight, now darkened by the scudding of fast-

181

moving clouds, Gunn saw that this was a place of primordial violence, of earthly upheaval, cosmic destruction. Huge slabs jutted up from the darkness, slanted as if jammed there by a giant hand. For several hundred yards around the gigantic cliff-face, there was nothing but rock, boulders, slabs, rocks. Nothing grew but scrub trees and small brush.

"There's the cave," said Fanny in a loud whisper.

"Dark as pitch," said Gunn. "Better let me go in there first, see if it's all right. I'll get a fire started."

"Yes," she said, relieved.

"How deep is it?"

"Very deep."

Dancing Star moaned. Fanny climbed down from behind Gunn. He withdrew his boot from the stirrup, offered his hand for the long drop. She held Gunn's helping hand for a long moment, but he could not see her face. Fanny hurried back to the travois. Distant thunder rumbled, and he saw the splash of light on the horizon. The storm was moving toward them. Soon the moon would be blotted out and he would have no light.

He fumbled in his saddle bags, found dry matches. He gathered dead brush as he walked gingerly through the pile of rocks, skirted boulders to reach the cave entrance. He moved cautiously inside. He walked slowly around the cave, feeling his way along its walls. The place smelled of wolf and bear, and his boots stepped in old scat.

But there was nothing there, and he knelt, made a small pyramid of the dry brush. He struck a match on the cave wall, watched it flare. He touched the flame to the wood. It caught and the fire crackled, grew, shooting sparks skyward. A large slab of rock served as the ceiling, two similar slabs jutted upward perpendicularly to form the walls. The cave was almost square, and Fanny had been right. It went backward a long way, farther than he could see. He stood up, walked outside to gather more firewood. The brush burned fast.

When the fire was going well, he hauled the travois inside the cave. While Fanny tended to Dancing Star, Gunn stripped Esquire, hobbled him and the Indian pony some distance from the cave where they could graze. It felt good to have the Winchester back. He cached the saddle and tack, lugged the saddlebags and rifle back to the cave.

"How is she?" he asked Fanny, as he set down the gear.

"Not very good. She's half-asleep, but I can see the pain moving through her."

He glanced at the Indian girl's face, the contorted features. She was drawn up on the travois-bed, her knees up around her belly. Her mouth was slack, her breathing very shallow.

"I'll fetch more wood," he said tightly.

Outside, the wind blew hard gusts, whipping at his shirt, his trousers. He had to jam his hat on to keep it from sailing away. He walked downslope, found rotted timber, brought back several pieces. Fanny had spread the blankets, made a bed for them. She had tended the fire well, and the cave was warm. Shadows flickered on the walls, the smoke flowed along the ceiling, was sucked outside by the growing wind.

Gunn made several trips until the deadwood was stacked high. Just as he stepped inside the cave with

183

the last load, a crackling bolt of lightning split the dark sky, flashed a sheet of white light across the moraine. Gunn's scalp tingled with the nearness of it and the air filled with the taste and smell of ozone, as if the pines had been fried by the electricity. A second later, the world plunged into darkness and the rain drove down violently, blotting out all but its own sound.

"Whew," exclaimed Gunn, as he set down the load of firewood. "Just in time." The rain lashed at the strewn rocks outside, and the firelight danced off its silver curtain.

"It looks like a waterfall," said Fanny, her voice thickened with fatigue.

He saw that her eyelids were droopy, and she could barely hold her head up.

"Some rain," he said laconically. "You'd better get some sleep."

"Yes, I'm very tired." She stretched out on the bedroll, looked at him with sleepy eyes.

"Did you ever stay here before?" he asked.

"Not inside. Pa came in here. It was daytime."

"Why?"

She hesitated, her eyes widening for a moment.

"I don't know," she said quickly. "Not exactly. He—he came here because of something Blood told him."

"Blood?" Gunn felt the fine hairs on the back of his neck crackle and rise.

Outside, peals of thunder rumbled across the landscape, and the rain came down in sheets. Lightning flared, close by, and when Gunn counted the seconds between lightning and thunder boom, they grew shorter. At a mile a second, the storm's electrical system went from 6 miles to a half mile, and then it did not move.

"Yes," she said, after a huge roar of thunder crashed, making her jump with fright. "Funny, I had almost forgotten that. Pa didn't like Blood much, didn't trust him, but he said something about this cave after Blood got drunk one night and talked about it."

"Do you remember what Blood said?" Gunn pressed.

Thunder crashed and it seemed as if the walls of the cave trembled. Its sound boomed as if magnified in the closeness of the shelter.

Fanny shook her head.

"I—I can't remember," she said.

"Try. Sleep on it," he told her. "It could be important."

"I'll try," she said, closing her eyes. A smile flickered on Gunn's lips. Fanny was already lost in slumber, dead to the world.

Gunn fed the fire, banked it for the night. He thought of the animals out there in the rain, was glad he had cached his tack under shelter. This was the kind of storm that could kill though. Flash floods, landslides, falling timber, lightning. These things could kill a man, an animal. It seemed, too, that the storm was stalled right above them.

Had they violated a sacred place by coming here? Or, were the Cheyenne right, as they were about so many things. That this was a place of evil spirits?

Gunn neither believed nor disbelieved. He listened, and he made judgments when necessary, based on his own observations. Beliefs shaped a man, he knew, and were important. He did not question other mens' beliefs, because for them, those beliefs worked, they made a foundation. He kept his own to himself and did not try to impress them on others. He knew there was a great spirit that moved through all things, something invisible and powerful, some seed-thing that seemed common to all life. And the Indians believed that everything was alive, like man, rocks, trees, water, air. And who was to say they were not right? Gunn thought perhaps that they might be right, that this was the secret to their being able to live close to the land and not have to cut, blast and scar the earth in order to live.

He puzzled over these thoughts because the fire crackled and the air outside turned white with lightning and the cave seemed, then, a special place where spirits, both good and evil, might gather if a man believed in such.

But behind these thoughts was another, a more nagging one. Blood. He knew of this place, had come here. Why?

Maybe the death of Jacques and Green Willow Leaf had not been an accident, an afterthought. Maybe Blood had deliberately killed them both. To capture Fanny, make himself look good to the Cheyennes. Yet there had to be something back of that, too. Blood wanted something. But was it only to be Cheyenne, to forsake the white world? Based on what Gunn knew of Blood, he doubted that. Red Cloud had won his war. There were no soldiers above the Platte on Sioux and Cheyenne lands. But something was brewing. Gunn knew that.

He just didn't know what, nor the reason.

But Blood knew.

Gunn shook his head, lay down next to Fanny. The noise of the thunder, the incessant spatter of rain blurred his thoughts, made him sleepy at last. He closed his eyes, and drifted down into the world of Morpheus. He did not hear the ominous rumble on the mountain, the terrible sound that was different from those made by the storm.

He did not hear the rocks loosen above the cave entrance, the first stones clattering downward, followed by earth and sand and larger ones.

Outside, the lightning crackled between clouds and earth, and a stub cedar, clinging precariously to the mountain, burst into flame, shook loose. Above it, a mass of rock shuddered and started its slow slide downward.

Chapter Nineteen

The moraine that slashed through the woods, cutting a wide swath, leaving the detritus of stone so deep that nothing would grow was actually caused by an ancient glacier. When it broke loose from its cradle on the mountain, it funneled downward leaving devastation in its wake. It smashed down trees, brought with it loosened boulders, tons of rock and hard-packed snow, snow that had been frozen for centuries.

Now with the hard rains, the deteriorated rock face, high above the cave entrance began to pulse with the pressure of water driving under its precarious moorings. The scrub cedar, its roots an octupus' tentacles in the earth, had been part of the complicated, delicate structure left behind from the avalanche. Now, scorched into ashes, its roots gouged out by wind-driven rain, it pulled loose from the mountain, tumbled down the cradle of stone, its sparks sputtering in the rainfall. Behind it, small stones burst loose from watered gravel, began sliding, gathering momentum, picking up speed. More and more loose stones joined the growing avalanche, weakening the base under the bigger boulders.

The mountain seemed to convulse as more and larger rocks, loosened, joined the floodtide that began the destruction of its face. A large slab sheared off, toppled into the bowl left by the ancient glacier. It struck with tons of force, smashing loose other stones and rock, splintering a mighty boulder in half with a crunching roar. The mass of stone shouldered down the slippery slope of the cradle, growing in size as it rammed loose tons of rock, prying mighty boulders out of sodden footings, pulling more and more of the mountain down behind its devastating onslaught. Picking up speed and mass, the rock roared down the mountain like a runaway locomotive, the friction setting off sparks, bursting plants into flame.

As the horrifying mass of earth and stone spread and grew, the sound became deafening. The mountain turned into a sheet of orange fire and could be seen for miles. In the Cheyenne camp, the people came out of their lodges to stand transfixed in the driving rain. They pointed to the mountain with its wall of flame, heard it rumble like an angry god, felt the earth shake beneath their feet.

"That is the once-sacred place," muttered a brave, and fell instantly dumb with a look of awe on his face.

The others muttered, and the women set up their trilling sounds as if they were about to die or as if a great grief had swept through the camp.

Little Wolf shook his medicine rattles, murmured a private incantation. Chief Old Bear summoned his men to council and ordered a tipi set up for purification ceremonies.

"This may not be good medicine," he said. "We must be careful."

The men grunted in assent and followed the old chief to his lodge. The rumbling continued as Yellow White Man's Fly, the medicine man, began chanting and dancing around in circles to appease the angry spirits.

Gunn awoke with a start, his ears shattered by Fanny's screams. He coughed, choked on dust clouds that rolled into the cave. The fire sputtered, gasped for oxygen under the smothering grit.

He could not see the cave entrance, but he heard the grinding smack of stone on stone, heard boulders crack and crumble as they struck the earth with enormous force.

The mountain rumbled and the cave floor shook with such violence that, at first, Gunn thought he was in the middle of an earthquake. He shook off the cobwebs of sleep, sat up. Fanny's face seemed a mask of horror as she whimpered, sat there, frozen.

"Fanny," he said. "Stop it."

She looked at him, wide-eyed in fear.

The Cheyenne woman did not awaken. Fanny drew her hands up into fists, choked and gasped on the dust, on her own hysteria.

"Gunn, I don't want to die."

"Save your breath," he said. "You may need it. I think there's a cave-in, or an avalanche." He had to yell in order to be heard above the roar. A calmness settled in him. This was not an earthquake, he reasoned. The ground did not roll under him as it would in such a cataclysm. His stomach did not roil and turn queasy with the kind of seasickness he had experienced during a San Francisco quake. No, this had to be something else. He listened, heard the tons of dirt and rock slide down the mountain with a roar like a thousand locomotives.

"It's a landslide," he yelled above the terrible sound.

"We're trapped," screamed Fanny.

Gunn did not reply, but already the air in the cave was becoming close. His lungs burned with every breath. He looked at the fire. A few small flames sputtered, flickered feebly, smothered by the lack of oxygen, the thick dust pouring into the cave. But the fire still burned.

Gunn's brows wrinkled in thought, creases appeared in his forehead. He moved toward the back of the cave, felt a strong draught just above his boot-tops. He lowered himself to the ground, breathed in clean air. He motioned for Fanny to come toward him.

"Lie flat on your stomach," he yelled into her ear. "You can breathe here. I'll bring Dancing Star over." He crawled toward the travois. The unconscious woman was covered with a fine patina of dust. Her breathing was very shallow. He wiped her face, dragged the makeshift litter toward the rear of the cave.

"Try and keep the dust off her, especially around the mouth and nostrils," he told Fanny.

"I — I'm scared."

"We'll be all right, I think," said Gunn. He hugged the floor of the cave, felt it tremble under his palms. The roar of sliding, crashing rock still boomed inside the cavern, but already showed signs of diminishing. His head ached now, even as the fire in his lungs began to quench with the fresh oxygen blowing in from the darkness beyond his vision.

They lay there for what seemed like hours. Suddenly, there was an enormous thundering crash and then a dead silence.

Fanny began to whimper, then broke into hysterical sobbing.

Gunn put a hand on her shoulder, gripped it firmly, tenderly. Her dress was covered with dust and grit. He wiped his face; his palms came away grimy. The fire sputtered as the dust settled.

Fanny stopped sobbing, twisted her head to look at Gunn.

"Is it over?" she asked.

"Maybe. Just lie still. Save your strength." Through the haze, he saw the boulders jammed into the entrance. He didn't want to tell Fanny, but he was sure that the avalanche had sealed off the opening to the cave. That would explain the shortage of fresh air from that direction, the absence of sky when he peered above the slowly settling dust at a point where the roof of the entrance ought to be. Some of the stones had rolled inside, rammed there by others.

A few pebbles rattled loose, giving Fanny a start. She turned around, looked at the cave entrance. A look of abject horror began to spread across her face.

"It's true," she stammered. "We're trapped alive in here."

She opened her mouth to scream.

That's when Gunn slapped her, hard across the mouth.

"You fall apart on me now," he said tightly, "we may never get out. Now, listen."

She stared at him, her eyes flashing with hatred, her lips quivering, her body shaking with a subdued rage.

"You bastard," she hissed. She touched a hand to her face, smoothed the burning trace of the slap.

Gunn grinned.

"Listen," he said again. "We can get out of here. It might take some time, but we can't lose our heads. We'll wait until the mountain settles down. If I start work now, it could trigger another landslide. But I'll start at the top, start moving rock."

"That could take days."

"Look at the bright side, Fanny. We're alive. We're breathing."

"You bastard," she said again, but Gunn's smile melted her, and she turned away quickly so he would not see that she was smiling too.

Gunn lay on his back, tasted dust on his lips. They were in a bad spot, he knew, but there was hope. If the rocks on top were not heavy, he might be able to dig out. In the darkness, it was difficult to tell. There was a small amount of air coming into the cave. Enough, he thought, to keep them alive. The fire still burned. That was a good sign. Perhaps there was another entrance to the cave. Perhaps there was a way out.

"We'll wait until the dust settles," he said. "Just stay still, breathe easy."

"We could be crushed to death."

"I don't think so. That was no earthquake. A landslide maybe."

"It sounded like the end of the world."

"Rain must have loosened some shale, decayed rock."

"You sound so calm, Gunn."

Inside, he was calm. It was always that way when things looked bad. Something inside him pulled all of his fear down into it, swallowed it up. The deadly calm. He had never questioned it. It kept him from losing his nerve. It had probably saved his life.

"It's the unknown that scares you," he replied.

Fanny grew quiet, lay there on her belly, breathing the air from an unknown source. The Indian girl, too, seemed at peace, her breathing steady, though shallow. Gunn touched her forehead. It was like touching a hot stove. He was sure her cheeks were cherry-red. That was good. The fever might burn the poison out of her. She needed care, though, medicine. She needed rest, her wounds tended to beyond what he and Fanny had been able to do.

Gradually, the dust inside the cave began to settle. As it did, as Gunn saw the massive blockages of rocks, a gloom settled in his heart. The pile looked solid, solid as an iron door in a jail cell.

He looked over at Fanny. Her eyes were closed. She was asleep. Gunn arose, selected a long branch, put its tip into the fire. He walked over to the mass of rock, climbed to the top. Touched a stone. It was still warm from its slide down the mountain. He pushed on it. The rock did not budge. He climbed over more stones, tested the rocks, looked for a loose one along the upper edge. They were all wedged in tight.

He scrambled down, checked the lower rocks, just in case. Solid.

"There's no way out, is there?" Fanny said bitterly.

Gunn was startled.

"I thought you were asleep."

"I can't sleep. It feels as if we're buried alive. I fall asleep and then I dream I'm choking to death, gasping for breath. Gunn, I don't want to die. Not like this."

"No," he said, as he sat beside her, took her in his arms. He rocked her gently, smoothed her hair away from her forehead with his hand. "You should not think of dying," he continued, "but of living. It looks bad right now, in the dark, but there has to be another way out. We're breathing good air. It has to be coming from the outside. In a while, when you're calmed down, I'll look for the passage that will get us out of here."

At that moment they both heard a terrible rumbling from above. There was the sickening sound of rock scraping on rock.

Then, it was quiet.

The cave was still.

The air turned stale all of a sudden.

The fire sputtered, flickered out as its source of oxygen shut off.

Gunn squeezed Fanny tightly before laying her back down on the cave floor.

"Don't leave me," she pleaded in the darkness.

But Gunn was already gone.

* * *

Little Wolf sat his pony, looked up at the place where the sacred cave had been. The mountain's base was bathed in mist, and rain still fell, plinking on the aspen leaves, rustling on the needles of pine and fir. Mosquitoes drifted up from the damp grasses, stirred from slumber by the pony's nervous hooves.

The brave made a sign and other Indians rode up warily, their torsos sleek with rainwater, their dark scalplocks drooping under beaded droplets. Yellow Dog, Bad Buffalo and Three Sticks stopped next to Little Wolf, who pointed to the place where the cave had been.

"Spirits have closed the door into the mountain," he said softly. His hand arced in a sweeping gesture. "Maybe the bad spirits have been locked in."

The others sat like stones atop their ponies. The ponies tossed their heads, shook water-sogged manes, pawed the earth with unshod hooves. Three Sticks looked down, saw something, rode off toward it. He followed a course, drawing Little Wolf's attention.

"What do you follow, little brother?"

"Travois tracks," said Three Sticks.

"Ho," said Little Wolf. "You have eyes like the hawk."

The others, when they leaned over, saw the faint marks that led to the cave entrance. They saw the tracks of the landslide, the mass of boulders that now blocked the entrance. Around them, trees were smashed flat where other large stones had hurtled down the mountain, plummeted beyond the ledges and roared through the woods. For several hundred feet in all directions, this was the way it was, and the Cheyenne had approached the once-holy mountain with fear and caution.

Three Sticks stopped, turned around.

"The tracks go into the mountain," he said. "A man pulled the travois."

"From where?" asked Bad Buffalo.

Three Sticks backtracked, followed the faint spoor. He disappeared behind a large boulder, but the others heard his pony break sticks in the woods.

Soon, they heard a shout.

"Hou!" exclaimed Three Sticks. "I have found horses."

The others rode after him, warily eyeing the mountain to the west of them. They rounded the boulder, saw the big sorrel, the Indian pony.

None spoke for a long time as the four braves carefully examined the ground for sign. They ranged in a wide circle, and made grunts as each new bit of evidence was discovered. Finally, they converged, the young men looking to the older Little Wolf to speak.

"This is very strange," he said. "We must tell Old Bear what we have found. We will take these horses back to the village. This big one is the horse of the gray-eyed white man. And this pony belongs to Dancing Star. The one called Fanny has been here, and she is the woman who walks. Dancing Star leaves no tracks. She rides the crossed sticks."

The young braves nodded, grunted their agreement of Little Wolf's words.

"They went into the mountain," he said. "And the mountain swallowed them up."

"We must tell the other people this," said Three Sticks.

"Yes," said Little Wolf. "This is a very strange thing

that has happened. Maybe it is a sign. Maybe strong medicine."

"The gray-eyed white man, maybe his spirit stays inside the mountain," said Bad Buffalo.

"And our sister, Dancing Star, sleeps there now," agreed Yellow Dog.

"The half-blood, Fanny, as well," said Three Sticks.

"These are deep secrets and we must ask Old Bear what to make of it," said Yellow Dog.

Esquire bobbed his head, shook his mane. He looked up at the mountain and whinnied long and loudly. His rubbery nostrils snorted, sending a spray of mist-soaked air toward the four braves. They looked at the animal in horror.

"Let us go," said Little Wolf. "Let us go quick."

The others were silent as they looked up at the mountain again. Yellow Dog caught up Esquire and the Indian pony, removed their hobbles.

Far off, they heard a distant rumble and the braves backed away from the mountain in fear. Overhead, thunder shook the clouds and the rain fell hard, making the trees clatter with sound.

The Indians rode off, then, and did not look back.

Chapter Twenty

Gunn groped blindly in the dark. On hands and knees, he crawled around the back of the cave, looking for the beginning of another passageway. His body was bathed in sweat, and his stomach quivered with a nameless fear. The air in the cave was lifeless, suffocating. He felt as if he was breathing his own expelled breath, dying slowly from an invisible gas. Bands of steel tightened around his chest, and his eyes burned from trying to peer through the impenetrable darkness.

He felt his way through an opening, hoped it was the right one. He stretched his arms out to his sides, felt the walls. He rose slowly, until he felt the ceiling touch his back just below the shoulder. A man could not stand fully upright, but there was room for him to walk if he hunched over slightly. He followed the passage by touching both walls, walked in a crouch. The floor of the tunnel was level for a time, rose slightly as he penetrated the mountain further.

A wisp of fresh air flicked over his nostril. Gunn gulped, drew in a deep breath, felt the searing heat in his lungs diminish. It was only a trickle, but the jet of oxygen gave him hope. He pushed on, felt the tunnel widen. The walls now, were so far apart, he felt he must be in a large cavern, a room as big as the one at the entrance. He stepped carefully, knowing there could be a downward shaft. He traversed the length of the room, felt the floor rise toward the thin stream of air. He began climbing, felt the cool breeze on his face. The slope was gradual, and the walls began to narrow again.

He felt his way up toward the air source, began breathing more easily the closer he came. He heard the patter of rain, and his heart started pumping hard. A flood of relief washed over him. His hand touched a small fissure above him. He touched a stone, jiggled it. He wanted to cry out, but knew that Fanny probably could not hear him. He wiped sweat from his forehead, stepped up to the crack, pushed at the stone with both hands. It tumbled away from the small opening, and rain splashed in his face.

He tasted the wetness on his tongue, savored the trickle of water that dripped into his open mouth. The stone, its purchase gone, fell away. Gunn tensed, afraid the fall might trigger another slide. The sound faded away and it was quiet, except for the rain falling outside, dripping heavy now, inside the cave. He climbed upward, pulled himself into the open air. It was lighter now, and on the horizon he saw a faint tinge of predawn light.

How long had they been in the cave? Hours, apparently. The avalanche had lasted a long time, and it seemed he had been crawling around in the dark for hours. He saw a streak of lightning crack the darkness. Seconds later, the thunderclap rolled over him, and he tensed again.

But there was no landslide this time, and he got a good glimpse of his surroundings when the lightning flashed.

He stood in the rain, somewhere beyond the blocked cave entrance, in a shallow depression. Scraggly cedars clung to the face of a nearby cliff, and the granite face of the backside of the mountain loomed above him, the other side sheared off by the avalanche.

Head tilted upward, his mouth open, Gunn breathed the rain-laden air, drew deeply as the water pelted him, washed his face, drenched his clothes, his body. Lightning whitewashed the sky, illuminated distant mountain peaks, quicksilvered the nearby crags. It was deadly to stay up here, he knew. Lightning sought the high points of the earth, traveled through stone and water. He could be electrocuted, fried like a waterbug, skinned like a tall tree if a bolt caught him. He had seen men knocked senseless by electric spears, heard calves scream and bawl when a streak of lightning had blistered their backs, scalped them to the backbone so that no hair ever grew. He had seen the white dust on the soles of dead men's feet — men who had been struck down, cooked inside like frogs on a spit.

He shuddered, took one last look at the land as another jagged scratch of silver lightened the land like an explosion of phosphor on a photographer's tray, and bent down to lower himself back into the cave.

Gunn descended into darkness, but the fresh wet

draughts of air blew at his back, gave him strength and courage. He knew what he had to do, but he knew it would not be easy.

Dancing Star listened to the faint tattoo of rain on the rock wall at the entrance of the cave. Her eyes brightened in the darkness, shone like the eyes of insects in bright sunlight. She quivered, broke free of unseen chains that bound her to the floor of the cavern. She shook off sickness and death, felt the awesome presence of spirits in the stifling black where she lay. She opened her mouth, but her breath was weak in her chest and would not force out the words her thoughts had made.

"Fanny," she croaked.

"Dancing Star?"

"Where are we? Am I alive?"

"You're alive," Fanny said, with relief. "We are in the spirit cave."

"And the gray-eyed white man?"

"I—I don't know. We couldn't breathe. He went to find a way out."

Fanny crawled to the side of the girl, touched her face in the darkness. The fever had broken; Dancing Star's brow was cool, her flesh clammy, the sweat on her forehead cold.

"I dreamed of a great wind and a loud thunder," said the injured girl. "It was dark and then it was light."

"Yes," Fanny sobbed, on the verge of hysteria. "Oh, yes." She patted Dancing Star's cheeks reassuringly, leaned over, hugged the wounded girl.

A coal in the fire winked, pulsed with an orange light as the breeze from the tunnel fanned it. A faggot burst into flame. The fire caught, blazed into life. Fanny watched it in fascination, then looked at Dancing Star, saw the shadows flicker over the Indian girl's face. Dancing Star smiled, struggled to rise.

"No, you shouldn't move," said Fanny quickly.

Dancing Star winced, ignored the warning. The pain was quiet now, distant. She sat, touched her tangled hair. She looked around the cave, its walls shimmering with golden light and shadows. She closed her eyes, opened them again, a smile flickering on her lips.

"I feel the spirits," she said.

Fanny's eyes widened, and she moved closer to Dancing Star, shivered involuntarily. The fire, whipped by the fresh breeze, blazed brightly now, filled the cavern with an unexpected warmth.

The women heard a noise, turned to see Gunn enter the cavern.

He dropped to his knees, looked at the two women.

"You look some better," he said to Dancing Star. "How do you feel?"

"Feel good."

"Strong enough to walk?"

"Walk, yes. Little."

"We can help her," he said to Fanny. "There's a way out. It's steep, be hard to climb the last part."

Fanny's face relaxed. She smiled.

"It's dark back there," said Gunn. "I'll take some light. Let's get Dancing Star on her feet. We'll have to leave the travois here. But once we get off this mountain, to the horses, we ought to be all right."

He and Fanny helped the Indian woman to her feet. Dancing Star stood shakily. The blood had dried and caked on her dress. She was wobbly, but Gunn thought she could make it if they took it slowly. Fanny supported the maiden, as Gunn took a stick out of the fire.

"This will give us some light," he said. "Let's go."

He helped the two women to the corridor leading from the main cavern, then struck out ahead of them. The breeze was stronger inside the tunnel. Now, with the light from the burning stick, Gunn could see where he had groped his way through.

A flash of light caught his eye as he held the torch over his head. He called a halt, stopped to examine a portion of the cave wall. He ran his fingers over the rough surface, dug a fingernail into the dull yellow vein that streaked the reddish layer of ferrous rock.

"Fanny," he said softly. "Come here a minute."

Fanny left Dancing Star leaning against the wall for support while she joined Gunn.

"Did your pa ever mention this?" he asked, pointing to the yellow vein in the iron-laden stone.

"What is it?"

Gunn drew his knife, gouged out a chunk of the yellow metal. He showed her the marks his fingernail had made.

"Gold," he said.

"Gold!" she exclaimed, breathless. "No, pa never said anything about it."

The vein was threaded through the rock, was nearly two inches in width. He saw other traces as he held the torch up higher.

"Unless I miss my guess, Jack Blood knows about

this," he said. "And your pa knew about it too."

"I don't understand."

Suddenly, it all seemed clear to Gunn. As he had suspected, there was more behind the raid on the wagons than at first met the eye. Jack Blood obviously wanted to curry favor with the Cheyennes under Chief Old Bear, but at the same time he had to get Jacques and Green Willow Leaf out of the way. They were probably the only two who knew of the vein of gold inside the sacred mountain. Besides Blood himself.

"Did your pa ever show any gold to you?"

Fanny shook her head.

"After he visited here, did he have money?"

She thought about it, then nodded somberly.

Gunn looked at the rest of the wall, saw the marks of a pick, sections of rock that had been hollowed out. So, Jacques had probably worked the cave, but never filed on it. He had not been greedy. How had Blood found out? Probably from Jacques himself. A moment of loose talk over a drink of whiskey, a dropped remark. Blood's ears would be attuned to such slips of the tongue. So Blood had killed the Frenchman, but that meant he had seen the gold for himself at one time. He believed, not hearsay, but direct evidence.

"Come on," said Gunn, "we have to find that Cheyenne camp before it's too late."

"Why? What's going on?"

"I think Blood meant to kill your pa and ma, and if he knows we've been in this cave, he'll want to kill you too."

Fanny shuddered.

* * *

Gunn climbed from the cave, tossed the burnt-down torch aside. It sputtered out in the rain. Dawn had slipped light through the dark clouds, giving a gray cast to the mountain, the stones. The hard rain limited visibility to a few yards. The tall man lay flat on his belly, called down to Fanny.

"You give Dancing Star a boost up. I'll pull her out."

"All right," said the half-breed girl.

"Think you can make it out?" Gunn asked the Indian maid.

"Yes."

The rain was cold on Gunn's back as he reached for Dancing Star's outstretched arms. Their fingers touched, and he clasped her hands, began to pull on her arms.

"Push," he told Fanny.

He heard a grunt, and reached down to grab Dancing Star's waist. He pulled her into his arms, rocked backward with her weight.

"Rest," he said. "I'll help Fanny."

"My sister is strong," said the girl, her face wet with rain. She flashed Gunn a sheepish smile and something inside him melted. Her clothing soon soaked through and the buckskin shirt clung to her breasts, outlined her graceful body. He shook off the feeling, crawled back over the exit hole. Fanny clambered upward and Gunn pulled her through the opening.

She sighed with relief, turned her face to the sky and drank the falling water.

"I've never been so happy in my life," she breathed.

"It seems as if we've just come out of hell."

Gunn laughed.

"We've still got a tough climb down. It'll be slippery, so watch your step."

He outlined a course of action. Lightning streaks made jagged rents in the lumbering dark clouds and thunder boomed across the crags of the mountain. They would have to climb over rimrock, avoid the talus slope where the landslide occurred. One slip, he knew, could trigger another avalanche. They could all be buried alive.

"Wait here a minute, while I look over the way down. When we go down, Dancing Star will go in the middle, hold onto my waist. You'll hold on to her waist, Fanny. Got that?"

"Yes. Gunn?"

"Yeah?"

"Thanks for getting us out."

He growled something, turned to scout the mountain. A large blunt spire rose above the small tunnel where they had emerged moments before. He climbed around it, saw the scar of the slide. He clung to the rock, backed away slowly. He saw a path in back of it that criss-crossed for fifty yards. That would have to be the way down. If he could hold his footing on the slick rock, they might make it. A few moments later, the trio took their first steps down the storm-damaged mountain.

The going was rough and slow. Gunn paused after each step, made sure of his footing before taking the next. Halfway down, the driving rain blurred the trail, and they took shelter behind a scraggly cedar. The noise blotted out the senses as the sun climbed, hidden deep beyond bulging clouds, struggled to push light through the dense cover. Lightning continued to flash and they shivered each time thunder threatened to jar them loose from their precarious perches on the side of the mount. A small river of mud and water coursed down the trail. The way, Gunn saw, was now even more treacherous than before.

Rain pelted his face as he continued cautiously down the steep slope. The trail wound around toward the slide area, and he had to backtrack, find another path. His calves ached from the strain of bending backwards, and Dancing Star gripped his waist so tightly, he felt the pinch of her fingers.

"Gunn, I—I can't go on," said Fanny.

"We have to. The water can wash us away at any time."

"I'm tired. Real tired."

"We will go on," said the exhausted Indian girl. Gunn could have kissed her.

The trail widened, became more clear-cut, and Gunn knew he had stumbled onto another switch-back leading away from the talus-slope where the slide had scraped off the face of the mountain. The going was easier now, but the water splashing off the rimrock was heavy. He felt as if someone was throwing huge buckets of water over them. The rain blinded him, clung to his mouth and nostrils, so that he had to bend his neck to breathe.

A flash of lightning, accompanied by a simultaneous boom of thunder, so loud it punched their eardrums, split open the sky. Gunn looked up, saw the electric bolt streak down, smash into the big boulder atop the mountain. The boulder burst apart, sent splinters of rock flying in all directions as if the rock had exploded. Deafened by the sound, he could barely hear the screams of the two women.

The mountain rumbled and rock began to slide from the top. Gunn felt the trail shake beneath his feet.

"Run!" he yelled above the roar.

He turned, jerked Dancing Star into his arms. Fanny pitched forward. He grabbed her under one armpit. He started dragging her down with him as he lunged off the path, plunged straight down the slope. Behind him, he heard the mountain rumble as the avalanche gained momentum. He did not dare look back, but scrambled on weakened legs toward a stand of thick aspen.

The roaring increased in his ears and when he gained the trees, he kept right on running, his feet moving slowly as if they were mired down in quick-sand.

The avalanche streamed downward, broke in two on a large craggy rock. Above it, the whole mountain shook, settled. A cloud of sparks and dust shot skyward over the entrance hole.

Gunn stopped, looked at the rain-shrouded mountain.

The other entrance, he knew, was now blocked off, maybe for eternity. Anyone wanting to go inside the mountain after the gold would have to blast their way inside. But the rock was unstable, and anyone tunneling in would have to use heavy beams to shore the tunnels.

Death hung in the air like a terrible reek.

The gold was hidden now, out of reach.

211

"Spirits," whispered Dancing Star, looking up at the mountain, her face splattered with rain.

"Yes," said Fanny softly, trying to catch her breath.

Gunn said nothing, but in the smoky rain he thought he could see the shapes of formless people, and in the dying echoes of the thunder, he heard old voices, strangely disembodied, chanting words he could not understand.

Chapter Twenty-one

No one had asked him about the mountain, but when Gunn and the women strode into the Cheyenne camp, they all looked at him in awe. Dripping wet, they had been taken to individual lodges to dry off. Gunn was put in a tipi by himself, and no one had visited him all day and into the night. Food was left outside the tipi's flap. He saw that his horse was decorated with feathers and beads, staked away from the pony herd in a place of honor. Then, when the night was dark, after the rain had stopped, the death dance began.

Gunn waited alone in the darkening tipi, listening to the threnodic thumping of the drums and the wails of the mourning Indians. Old Bear and the braves of the tribe danced in a frenzy, demonstrating their grief for the slain Red Arrow. The women's screams floated through the camp, their shrill voices trilling their keening cry, their bodies undulating in a dancing lamentation for the dead. For almost three hours now, the drums and the droning cries had thrummed on Gunn's nerves.

His senses heightened by the fever pitch of the mourners, Gunn's hand slapped for his pistol at the rustle outside the tent. Fanny slipped easily through the tipi opening.

The man stopped his weapon in mid-air to watch the lovely half-breed come forward into the flickering firelight. Her long black hair was smoothed in the Indian style, a hide strip at her brow and braided into two long plaits that fell to below her breasts.

"Gunn," the girl spoke softly. "I don't like what Running Deer is doing."

"What's that?" the man responded.

"He left the dancing and took off to the clearing where Jack Blood is tied."

Without further questioning, Gunn rose and swiftly crossed the space to the tent opening. There were no guards outside the flap. Chief Old Bear trusted the white man to stay in the camp, apparently. It was odd, but he knew there must be much behind it. Perhaps Dancing Star or Fanny had said something, had told the story of the mountain. Still, he felt odd, almost like a ghost among the living.

Not breaking his stride, Gunn gained the clearing where Blood was tied. The rising moon lighted the open space, casting a long shadow around the lone lodge pole. Jack Blood was nowhere in sight.

Gunn examined the bit of leather that hung from the stake. The rawhide had been sliced clean. Running Deer had freed Jack Blood.

It didn't make sense. The young brave hated Blood for the humiliation the prisoner had caused the Indian. Several warriors had laughed about the times that Blood had caused the boy pain, shame.

Fanny stood beside the tall man in the clearing. "Why would he let Blood go, Gunn? It doesn't make sense."

"Maybe he didn't let him go, Fanny. Maybe the boy carries so much hatred that he wanted Blood all for himself." Gunn searched the moonlit ground for sign, direction.

"We better find the boy before Jack Blood hurts him and gets away." The man squatted over some footprints in the dust at the edge of the clearing.

"Fanny, go tell Old Bear. Send him over this way." The tall man stood and pointed in the direction of the river. "I'm going after them before the boy gets himself killed."

The sounds of the screaming Indians faded as Gunn crept softly in the direction that the footprints led him. He could hear the splashing of the river ahead of him. Another sound echoed above the rush of the water. He heard the slap of flesh against flesh, the grunts of men scuffling.

The brush fell away from the edge of the river allowing the moon to glance off the white stones along the bank. Gunn could see them now. Blood and Running Deer were flailing at each other, standing toe to toe in the white rock at the edge of the river bed.

Gunn eased his pistol out of its holster, cocked the hammer silently by holding the trigger in slightly.

215

"Hold it, Blood!" Gunn stepped forward, the moonlight glared off the barrel of his gun.

Running Deer's head popped up and he lowered his fists, letting his guard down. Blood let a smashing blow fly into the boy's face, sent the brave down, crumpled into unconsciousness.

Blood's hands fell to his side. "You're a brave one, Gunn, with that forty-five talking for you."

Gunn slid his pistol back into its holster, eased the hammer down.

"We've got a fight to finish, Blood." Gunn unlatched his buckle and let his gunbelt fall to the ground. The bone-handled Mexican knife eased out of its sheath and glistened under the glare of the moon.

Blood stepped to Running Deer's side and slipped the boy's knife out of its buckskin sheath.

The two men stared at each other and began to circle slowly, each watching the other's eyes for signs of attack. The smooth rocks clattered under Blood's boot as the killer lunged toward Gunn. Gunn jumped backward, felt the Indian blade slice the air inches away from his chest.

The tall man rushed the half-breed, brought the knife arcing downward. Blood slid out from under the motion, jabbed at Gunn too late.

Gunn stepped back as Blood lunged again, going for the kill. The half-breed's knife slashed at Gunn's throat. The tall man reached up, grabbed Blood's wrist, stopping the blade. For a moment, the two men stared at each other, braced for anything that might happen.

The breed's free hand locked around Gunn's knife-wielding fist. The two pushed, strained, holding each other back through sheer effort of wills and muscles. The knife inched closer to Gunn's throat.

Gunn lashed out with his boot, tripped the attacker, breaking his grip. Blood cried out at the sudden, sharp pain in his shin.

The two enemies rolled, locked together, crunching the gravel under their weight. Jack Blood, summoning his strength in one mighty effort, came out on top with his knife poised to kill the white man who had caused him so much trouble. Blood's face froze with a leer of hatred as he anticipated his moment of revenge. He hesitated, his visage a mask of rage.

"You sonofabitch, I kill you," Blood panted.

"That gold is buried under a hundred ton of rock," said Gunn.

"What?"

"The gold you killed Jacques and Green Willow Leaf for."

"You lie!" Blood spat.

"I was there. I saw the vein. I saw the mountain come down on top of it. Both entrances are sealed up like a tomb."

"Motherfucker," hissed Blood. "Lying bastard . . ."

Blood lunged, sure of his prey. Sure that he could cut out Gunn's throat, take his scalp to hang on his belt.

The half-breed underestimated the skill and agility

217

of the white man. Gunn grabbed Blood's wrists, the muscles on his arms quivering, the veins standing out in bluish cords. Gunn pushed the breed backward, shoving the man from atop him. Gunn swung himself upright as Blood rolled to his feet and lunged toward the white man. Gunn swung his blade in a wide, slashing arc, slammed it into Blood's gut, just above his belt buckle. Blood grunted in pain, dropped his weapon. Both the breed's hands closed on the handle of the knife that protruded from his belly. He lifted his head to stare at Gunn, a puzzled look in his frightened eyes. Blood doubled over, pitched head-long onto the ground.

Gunn stared at the fallen man, watched the blood form on the rocks where Jack Blood lay. The tall man reached down and tugged the Mexican knife from the breed's gut. He rammed the blade deep into the gravel, cleaned it in the deep layer of sand.

An odd hush fell over the place and Gunn realized that the dancing had stopped, the screaming of the women had silenced.

"The spirits are satisfied, Gunn. The three braves will walk easy in the sky now that Jack Blood is dead." Chief Old Bear's voice broke the stillness.

Gunn turned to look at the old man and watched, his brow furrowed in wonder, as two braves laid Dancing Star's litter on the river bank. So, he thought, the Cheyenne have tended to her, begun the deep healing that was needed. He wondered, though, how she had managed to walk out of the mountain. It was not until they had come to the camp that she had

218

collapsed again, that he realized how serious her wounds were.

Old Bear took Gunn's knife from him, walked to Blood's body. He knelt, gouged out both of the dead man's eyes. He threw the orbs into the river. They landed *kerplunk*, disappeared. The old man said something Gunn could not understand, then turned to him. He handed Gunn back his knife.

"My daughter has come to the river to die. She would speak to us, Gunn. Come."

Gunn sheathed his knife, followed the old chief.

Old Bear squatted beside his youngest daughter.

"Did you speak with the spirits, my daughter?"

"Yes, Father." The girl's voice was weak, could hardly be heard above the rushing of the water. "They told me to listen to the blood on Green Willow Leaf's beaded necklace, the one I gave her many winters ago."

"Did the blood speak to you, my daughter?"

"Yes, Father. The blood of my sister, Green Willow Leaf, said to listen to the gray-eyed man. He speaks with straight tongue."

"It is what we know now, my daughter. Jack Blood is dead. His spirit is bad. It will not rest, but roam the endless sky alone, always searching, but never finding peace. He has no eyes to see and his spirit will not find a place to live forever."

Gunn heard the words and understood now why Dancing Star did not speak up right away.

"I would speak to the white man, Gunn, my father."

Gunn crouched down beside the litter.

Dancing Star smiled and reached for Gunn, took his hand in hers.

"You understand me now, Gunn. Understand the way of the Cheyenne."

The man nodded, gripped the dying woman's hand tightly.

"Where is my sister's daughter?"

"I'm here, Dancing Star." Fanny stepped from among the women who had gathered near the litter.

"Come here, my little Cheyenne sister." Dancing Star gestured to the girl with her hand. Fanny sat down upon the rocks at Gunn's side and held out her hand to the dying woman.

Dancing Star took the girl's hand in hers and looked from Gunn to Fanny. The woman brought the hands of the man and the girl together, held them firmly in her own. She turned Gunn's fist palm up and placed Fanny's hand into the roughened one.

"Go in peace together. Green Willow Leaf is pleased with you."

The dying woman looked at her father, then turned her eyes beyond the gathered crowd, to the sky.

"I go now to see Green Willow Leaf, my father. I am happy this night. My life is full and I die happy." Dancing Star exhaled slowly, quietly and closed her eyes.

Their hands still clasped, Fanny and Gunn looked at each other for a long time. The pair rose as the huddle of Cheyenne onlookers began to separate, drift away from the chief's dead daughter.

"You can stay here, you know," Gunn said.

"I know."

"You have no folks, but these."

Fanny watched the departing Indians, then looked down at the body of her dead aunt lying there in the white buckskin.

"Take me home, Gunn," she whispered.

"Where is home, Fanny?"

"Wherever you go, Gunn."

The man swallowed hard, fought back a mist welling in his eyes.

He tried to speak, no words came out. There was nothing for him to say anyway. Not now.

Gunn drew a deep breath, took Fanny in his arms and gripped her tightly to him.

The keening trill of the women drowned out his thought. A great sadness swept through the camp. These Cheyenne had lost four strong people. Gunn would miss them, Red Arrow and Dancing Star.

The couple walked slowly back toward the village, their arms at each others' waists. The clouds still lingered. One lone star sat over the gray horizon. Dawn seemed just beyond its scintillating light, a paleness to the eastern horizon, an illusion, perhaps. Fanny pointed toward the sky.

"See?" she said, as the trilling stopped.

The sky opened up and the pale cream of dawn leaked out, began to spread.

Gunn saw it, and the hackles rose on the back of his neck. They both stared. The Cheyenne stopped and gazed toward the dawn. They all saw it.

Fanny drew closer to him, to the shelter of his embracing arm.

"Her spirit has gone to the good place," said Fanny softly.

The morning star shone with a brilliant light.

And the star was dancing.

WHITE SQUAW
Zebra's Adult Western Series
by E.J. Hunter

#1: SIOUX WILDFIRE   (1205, $2.50)

#2: BOOMTOWN BUST   (1286, $2.50)

#3: VIRGIN TERRITORY   (1314, $2.50)

#4: HOT TEXAS TAIL   (1359, $2.50)

#5: BUCKSKIN BOMBSHELL   (1410, $2.50)

#6: DAKOTA SQUEEZE   (1479, $2.50)

#7: ABILENE TIGHT SPOT   (1562, $2.50)

#8: HORN OF PLENTY   (1649, $2.50)

#9: TWIN PEAKS — OR BUST   (1746, $2.50)

Available wherever paperbacks are sold, or order direct from the Publisher. Send cover price plus 50¢ per copy for mailing and handling to Zebra Books, Dept. 1773, 475 Park Avenue South, New York, N.Y. 10016. DO NOT SEND CASH.

THE NEWEST ADVENTURES AND ESCAPADES OF BOLT
by Cort Martin

#11: THE LAST BORDELLO   (1224, $2.25)
A working girl in Angel's camp doesn't stand a chance—unless Jared Bolt takes up arms to bring a little peace to the town . . . and discovers that the trouble is caused by a woman who used to do the same!

#12: THE HANGTOWN HARLOTS   (1274, $2.25)
When the miners come to town, the local girls are used to having wild parties, but events are turning ugly . . . and murderous. Jared Bolt knows the trade of tricking better than anyone, though, and is always the first to come to a lady in need . . .

#13: MONTANA MISTRESS   (1316, $2.25)
Roland Cameron owns the local bank, the sheriff, and the town— and he thinks he owns the sensuous saloon singer, Charity, as well. But the moment Bolt and Charity eye each other there's fire—especially gunfire!

#14: VIRGINIA CITY VIRGIN   (1360, $2.25)
When Katie's bawdy house holds a high stakes raffle, Bolt figures to take a chance. It's winner take all—and the prize is a budding nineteen year old virgin! But there's a passle of gun-toting folks who'd rather see Bolt in a coffin than in the virgin's bed!

#15: BORDELLO BACKSHOOTER   (1411, $2.25)
Nobody has ever seen the face of curvaceous Cherry Bonner, the mysterious madam of the bawdiest bordello in Cheyenne. When Bolt keeps a pimp with big ideas and a terrible temper from having his way with Cherry, gunfire flares and a gambling man would bet on murder: Bolt's!

#16: HARDCASE HUSSY   (1513, $2.25)
Traveling to set up his next bordello, Bolt is surrounded by six prime ladies of the evening. But just as Bolt is about to explore this lovely terrain, their stagecoach is ambushed by the murdering Beeler gang, bucking to be in Bolt's position!